"Cody, You're Expected To Sleep Here With Me, Aren't You?"

Carina asked.

"That's the general idea," Cody told her.

"You would be very embarrassed to have to find another place to spend the night, wouldn't you?"

"I'm sure I'd survive," he drawled. "Is that what you want me to do?"

She looked down at her hands. "I don't want to do anything that will cause you problems."

He placed his hands on her shoulders and waited until she lifted her eyes and their gazes met.

"Carina, I know that you don't know much about men and marriage. So what I need to do is to let you get used to sharing your life with a man."

He took a deep breath. "Sooner or later we *are* going to become intimate."

D1115649

Dear Reader,

November is a time for giving thanks, and this year I have an awful lot to be thankful for—my family, my friends and my terrific job. Because it's through my job that I get to bring to you, the readers, books written by fabulous authors. These are love stories that will give you a lift when you're down, that will make you laugh and cry and rediscover the unique joy of falling in love.

This November has so *many* wonderful stories, starting with the latest in Annette Broadrick's SONS OF TEXAS series, *Marriage Texas Style!* (If you missed the earlier SONS OF TEXAS, don't worry, because this volume also stands alone.)

Next, there's our *Man of the Month* ex-sky jockey Kyle Gordon. Kyle is cocky, opinionated, sexy—altogether he's perfect, and he more than meets his match in schoolteacher Susan Brooks.

November is completed with Barbara Boswell's *Double Trouble* (don't ask me to explain the plot—just read the book), Joan Johnston's *Honey and the Hired Hand*, Doreen Owens Malek's *Arrow in the Snow* (welcome back, Doreen!), and Leslie Davis Guccione's *A Rock and a Hard Place*.

So take time from your busy holiday schedule to curl up with a good Desire book. I know I'm going to!

All the best,

Lucia Macro
Senior Editor

ANNETTE BROADRICK

MARRIAGE TEXAS STYLE!

SILHOUETTE *Desire*®

Published by Silhouette Books New York

America's Publisher of Contemporary Romance

SILHOUETTE BOOKS
300 East 42nd St., New York, N.Y. 10017

MARRIAGE TEXAS STYLE!

ISBN: 0-373-05745-8

First Silhouette Books printing November 1992

All the characters in this book have no existence
outside the imagination of the author and have
no relation whatsoever to anyone bearing the same
name or names. They are not even distantly
inspired by any individual known or unknown
to the author, and all incidents are pure invention.

Printed in the U.S.A.

Books by Annette Broadrick

Silhouette Desire

Hunter's Prey #185
Bachelor Father #219
Hawk's Flight #242
Deceptions #272
Choices #283
Heat of the Night #314
Made in Heaven #336
Return to Yesterday #360
Adam's Story #367
Momentary Marriage #414
With All My Heart #433
A Touch of Spring #464
Irresistible #499
A Loving Spirit #552
Candlelight for Two #577
Lone Wolf #666
Where There Is Love #714
**Love Texas Style!* #734
**Courtship Texas Style!* #739
**Marriage Texas Style!* #745

Silhouette Romance

Circumstantial Evidence #329
Provocative Peril #359
Sound of Summer #412
Unheavenly Angel #442
Strange Enchantment #501
Mystery Lover #533
That's What Friends Are For #544
Come Be My Love #609
A Love Remembered #676
Married?! #742
The Gemini Man #796

Silhouette Books

Silhouette Christmas Stories 1988
"Christmas Magic"

*Sons of Texas

ANNETTE BROADRICK

lives on the shores of the Lake of the Ozarks in Missouri, where she spends her time doing what she loves most—reading and writing romance fiction. Since 1984, when her first book was published, Annette has been delighting her readers with her imaginative and innovative style. In addition to being nominated by *Romantic Times* magazine as one of the Best New Authors of that year, she has also won the *Romantic Times* Reviewer's Choice Award for Best in its Series for *Heat of the Night, Mystery Lover* and *Irresistible,* the *Romantic Times* WISH Award for her hero in *Strange Enchantment* and the *Romantic Times* Lifetime Achievement Award for Series Romance.

Prologue

Cody Callaway slipped inside the rear door of the crowded church. He wasn't surprised to see that the event had the pews packed tightly. After a quick glance around the room, he leaned against the back wall and folded his arms. The bride and the groom were already at the altar. The minister began to speak.

"Dearly beloved..."

Cody gave a silent sigh of relief. At least he had gotten here in time for the actual ceremony. Absently, he felt the knot of his tie to make certain it was still in place. He was not a suit-and-tie man. He could count on one hand the number of times he had gotten dressed up like this. He kept his gaze on the couple standing before the minister.

Funerals and weddings. Strange how a person was supposed to dress more formally at such times. He'd been to his share of funerals, unfortunately. A wedding was a much more pleasant reason to dig out his respectable clothes.

He searched the wedding party and recognized most of the faces. His oldest brother, Cole, stood by the groom, obviously filling the position of best man for his brother Cameron.

Cole's wife, Allison, was one of the attendants for the bride.

In one of the first few rows he saw his Aunt Letitia, dabbing at her eyes. Was it possible the woman had a heart beneath that stiff exterior? His gaze swept over the attendants, then darted back to one face in particular. His twenty-year-old nephew, Tony, stood there, almost as tall as his father, Cole. My God, wasn't the kid ever going to stop growing?

The sonorous voice of the minister continued.

His family. Cody struggled to handle the emotion that welled up inside him. He had almost missed a very important occasion in the history of his family—his brother Cameron's wedding. As much as he resented the media's intense interest in anything and everything the Callaways did, if news of the wedding hadn't been splashed all over the newspapers when he crossed into McAllen, Texas, from Mexico that morning he would never have known about the event until it was too late to attend.

Even so, he had almost missed it. He had driven like a bat out of hell to reach the Circle C Ranch—the family's headquarters—only to discover that his aunt and most of the ranch help had already left. He had searched for and found the suit that he had worn at Cole's wedding...when was that? Five years ago...six?

He had seen very little of his family during the past few years; he had seen nothing of them in the past six months. He knew that he would hear plenty on that subject after the wedding. He smiled to himself. There was something pleasurable in being able to predict his family's reactions. He would feel that he was truly back home once the family began cataloging his many irritating traits...such as disappearing without a trace for months at a time.

He watched Cameron slip a ring on his bride's finger. Janine looked radiant standing there beside his tall brother, Cody thought. Cody had met her last spring, as he recalled, the same weekend that Cameron had met her. Even then, he had seen the sparks fly between the two of them. He shouldn't have been surprised at the outcome.

Movement near the bride caught his eye, and Cody saw Cameron's six-year-old daughter fussing with her ruffled dress. He was comforted by the thought that Trisha now had a mother. From the adoring glances she continued to give her former preschool teacher, Cody guessed she was quite pleased with the situation.

Thank God, Cameron had found a new love. When his wife, Andrea, was killed in the accident that almost took Cameron's life, Cody and Cole had worried that Cameron would never snap out of the despair he had experienced. The accident had been no accident, in Cody's mind. A similar mishap had killed both of his parents many years before. Cody had never believed in coincidences.

Following up on years of old leads had led him to spending most of his time south of the Texas-Mexico border. Without knowing about the wedding, he had returned north to discuss his latest findings with Cole. Thank God, he hadn't postponed the trip another day.

He had missed his family more than he would have thought possible. Orphaned at ten, Cody had learned through necessity to be self-reliant and self-sufficient. Although he had two older brothers and an overbearing aunt, Cody had learned to go his own way for almost twenty years now. He knew that part of his independence had been due to the unholy glee he felt in irritating and thwarting Aunt Letty's need to dominate and control those around her. His independence eventually became a habit...a way of life.

Cody watched as Cameron slipped his arm around Janine and leaned down to kiss her. His tenderness touched Cody as nothing else had in a long time. His brothers had found happiness in relationships that evolved into marriage. Cody could almost envy that closeness, except that he knew he would be stifled in a similar relationship.

What worked for Cole and Cameron would never work for him. He treasured his freedom too much. However, he could celebrate their happiness with his family. For this little while, he could include himself in the Callaway family circle.

The swell of a triumphant wedding march filled the church. The spectators stood and watched the happy couple start up the aisle toward the exit near where Cody stood. He wasn't certain what caught Cameron's eye, but his brother glanced in his direction. The wide grin of recognition and joy at his presence caused a lump to form in Cody's throat. What was it about weddings that tugged at people's emotions? He gave Cameron a thumbs-up sign of approval and a smile.

By the time the wedding party and all the onlookers and well-wishers had emptied out of the church,

Cody had been spotted by several members of the family.

"Uncle Cody! Uncle Cody! You came!" Trisha came tearing across the sidewalk and flung herself at him.

He lifted her high into his arms and was rewarded by a life-threatening squeeze around his neck. "You look like a princess, sweetheart," he managed to say when he could get some wind back into his lungs.

She patted her dress. "I know," she admitted with a great deal of satisfaction, causing Cody to laugh.

A deep voice interrupted him. "I'm glad you were able to make it today," Cole said, holding out his hand. Cody ignored the offering and threw his other arm around his brother. "It's good to see you, Cole. I'm glad I could be here." He could see the color flood his brother's face. Cole had always had trouble with public displays of affection. Flashbulbs were going off all around them. Cody grinned, thinking about possible captions that might accompany such a picture.

"I did everything I could to find you," Cole admitted. "You've got a damn good way of disappearing."

Cody nodded. "I didn't mean to stay away so long, Cole. The past six months have been crazy. I've managed to get some information that you'll want to hear, once we have a little privacy." He hitched Trisha higher on his hip for emphasis. Glancing around at the milling people, he said, "Allison looks great. Didn't you mention something about expecting twins the last time we talked?"

Trisha clapped her hands. "Oh, yes, Uncle Cody! Katie has two little bitty brothers called Clint and Cade. They make funny faces and gurgly sounds, and once I got to hold Clint."

Cole's grin was filled with pride. "We left the twins in Austin with their nurse. Allison had all she could handle today with Katie." The two men glanced over to where Allison stood visiting with some of the local people, her small daughter bouncing by her side as if she were on a pogo stick.

"How old are they now?" Cody asked.

"Almost three months. They were a little early but, thank God, they were all right." He lifted a brow and drawled, "You think you could hang around long enough to be introduced to them?"

Cody met his brother's level gaze. "Not this time, I'm afraid. I've got to head back south in a few hours. I came up to see you, but I didn't expect to find you at a wedding." He glanced across the church grounds at Cameron and Janine. "I'm so glad I managed to get here. Seeing Cameron happy again was worth the effort."

"How did you hear about the wedding, anyway?"

Cody grinned. "Can a Callaway do anything in this state without it being reported in some fashion? I happened to pick up a paper when I stopped in McAllen for coffee."

"So none of my messages reached you?"

Cody shook his head.

"I don't like it, Cody. I'm not trying to pry into your affairs, dammit, but it wouldn't be asking all that much to have some way to contact you in an emergency, now, would it?"

"Shame on you, Uncle Cole. You aren't supposed to cuss," Trisha pointed out sternly.

"So I'm told," Cole admitted with a sheepish grin. "I do humbly apologize, Miss Callaway."

"Well, just don't do it again," she replied in her best schoolmarm voice.

Both men laughed at her perfect mimicry of their Aunt Letty.

"Cody!" Allison had spotted him and was hurrying to him, Katie clutched in her arms. Heads turned in his direction and Cody almost winced. He had never cared for the attention being a Callaway drew, even though he had eventually learned to deal with the inevitability of public exposure. He schooled his expression to reveal nothing of his discomfort, lowering Trisha to the sidewalk just in time to catch his petite sister-in-law in his arms. "Oh, Cody!" Tears made her black eyes glisten. "We've been so worried about you! I'm so glad you made it." She gave him a ferocious hug. "Have you met Janine yet?"

He hugged her back. "I met her the same weekend Cameron did, last spring. I'm glad to see they made a match of it. It's good to see him smiling again."

She laughed. "Now you're the last holdout in the family, Cody. We're going to have to find you a wife!"

He shook his head, not having to simulate horror. "No way, Allison. I think it's great Cole and Cameron are married. Cole seems to be singlehandedly populating the region with Callaways." He grinned when she blushed. "I'm just not the marrying kind."

"Well," she replied, cocking her head, "I must admit that a wife would want to see you more than once or twice a year."

Before Cody could reply, he heard Cole mutter under his breath, "Brace yourself, bro. Here comes Aunt Letty." They looked at each other, recognizing their shared response toward the woman marching over to him.

Cody sighed. He would rather be engaged in battle with a gang of Mexican bandits than deal with the woman who had been in charge of him for so many years.

Family. That was what it was all about. You could love 'em, fight with 'em, leave 'em and marry 'em off. Regardless, you stood by them, just as Cole was doing now. He might give his brother hell, but he would defend him whenever anyone else attempted to do the same.

Family. What would he do without them?

Several hours later, Cody and Cole sat in the study located in the Big House at the Circle C Ranch. Cody had to admire the way his brother cleared the way for the two of them to leave the reception early so they could get back to the ranch and talk.

At the moment they were enjoying a couple of belated congratulatory cigars. Their coats and ties had been discarded and a crystal decanter of bourbon sat between them on the desk.

"So what have you got?" Cole asked.

Cody studied the ash that clung to the end of his very expensive cigar. "Does the name Enrique Rodriguez mean anything to you?" he finally asked, looking up at his brother.

"That's a rather common name in this part of the country, Cody. You know that."

"Yeah, I know. Let's go back to a little family history. When our ancestor, Caleb Callaway, came to Texas, he managed to acquire this ranch from a Spanish don whose family had lived here for several generations."

Cole gave him a sharp look. "The Rodriguez family."

"That's correct."

"Do you think there's some link between the thievery, accidents and anonymous threats we've been experiencing at some of our companies and that ancient history?"

"I believe there's a strong possibility. I've talked with many people in the past few years, in an effort to get to the bottom of all these seemingly unrelated incidents. What has slowly emerged is a psychological profile of a person filled with bitterness, resentment and hatred toward anyone or anything connected with the Callaways. About six months ago, I was given the name Enrique Rodriguez. In finding out more about him, I discovered that he's a direct descendant of the family that originally owned the ranch."

"Good God, Cody. The Callaways acquired this land almost a hundred years ago. How could someone still be holding a grudge?"

"Enrique, or Kiki as his friends call him, seems to hold the Callaway family responsible for every bad thing that ever happened to him since he was born. He was fed all of the family bitterness and resentment along with his mother's milk. Every time we get mentioned in the news, more fuel is added, because his family's fortunes have continued to deteriorate over the years."

"Didn't Caleb win the place in a game of cards?"

"That's the story I always heard."

"Is this Enrique accusing the Callaways of stealing the land?"

"I don't think he's gone quite that far, but then, again, I wouldn't put it past him."

"How old is he?"

"In his forties." Cody leaned forward, resting his elbows on his knees. "I think Enrique may be responsible for the accident that killed Andrea and almost killed Cameron five years ago."

Cole carefully set his glass down. "The accident we never quite believed was an accident," he murmured. "Then we were right in our suspicions."

"From what I've been able to find out from my contacts, the man is capable of the act, and he was seen in the area during that time."

Cole caught the part Cody had hoped to gloss over. "Your contacts," he repeated, in a level tone of voice that didn't fool Cody in the least.

Cody sighed. Even though he had received permission from his immediate superior, he didn't relish telling Cole what he had been doing for the past four years.

So he hedged. "You know how it is. I come into contact with all kinds of people when I'm out roaming the countryside."

"Ah. You must be talking about your well-known reputation—how you've made a career out of being the wild, youngest son—the one who runs with the fastest crowds, drives the flashiest cars, and is seen with the most glamourous women."

The ten-year age difference between them had never seemed so wide to Cody. He understood that gulf much better now that he was an adult. It was more than age—it was the vast difference in their life experiences. Cole had been forced by circumstances to take on tremendous responsibilities by the time he was twenty, forced to mature before he'd had an opportunity to enjoy the life of the oldest son of a privileged family. Cody had never envied Cole his role in the family dynasty. The responsibilities thrust upon Cole would have destroyed a lesser man.

"Is this where you're going to lecture me on my wasted life?" he asked Cole, with a wry grin.

Cole took a sip of his whiskey before replying. "I might, if I believed it."

Cody straightened, staring at the older man. "What's that supposed to mean?"

"I don't know what you're really up to, Cody, but I don't believe this reputation you've gone to such pains to build up. I know you too well. There are too many unexplained absences in your life, between bouts of lavish living and conspicuous consumption. Would you be willing to enlighten me on what's been going on?"

Cody felt like a schoolboy who thought he had been getting away with something, only to discover the teacher had known what he was doing all along. Thankful for the clearance he had received earlier from his boss, he said, "I've been using my reputation to cover my activities along the border."

"Which are?"

"I'm working with the DEA."

Cole froze, his eyes narrowing. "The hell you are. Since when?"

"Almost four years."

"Four years! You mean all this time you've been pretending to— Then all these parties and—"

Cody couldn't recall ever seeing Cole at a loss for words before. Even though Cole admittedly had suspected something didn't quite ring true about Cody's life-style, obviously he hadn't come close to guessing the truth. Cody savored the moment. He found it re-

assuring to know that even Cole could be rattled upon
occasion. Somehow it made him endearingly human.

"The agency suggested we use my playboy image as
a cover. It's been a good one. My name has opened
doors to many places that another agent could not
have managed."

"No wonder I haven't been able to find you," Cole
murmured almost to himself after a few minutes.

"You're right that you need to know where to contact me in case of an emergency. I'll give you a number to call."

"So you're working in Mexico."

"For the most part, yes. I'm working with several
agents, some with our government, others are with the
Mexican government. I'm doing everything I can to
stem the flow of drugs across the border."

"Is this Enrique involved with drug smuggling?"

"I can't tell at this point. My investigation of him
has had to be done in my spare time. I was fortunate
to find out that he has been seen in the area I'm
working. That was an unexpected break."

"So what are you going to do now?"

"I've got to get back. There's a series of meetings
I'm to attend that may break the case we've been
working on for the last couple of years. However, I
wanted to get Enrique's name to you. If something
should happen to me, I want you to follow up on my
investigation."

"Are things heating up for you?"

"Enough."

"Is what you are doing worth risking your life for?"

"I think so."

Cole slowly stood up and held out his hand. Cody stood and clasped his brother's hand in a firm grip. "If I can help, let me know," Cole said quietly.

"You already have, by just listening. I finally received clearance to tell you what I'm doing. One of the big honchos in D.C. went to school with you and considers you trustworthy."

"Glad to hear it," Cole drawled. He punched Cody's shoulder. "Keep in touch as much as you can, will you?"

"I'll do my best."

Cody walked out of the study, down the wide hallway to the massive front door. He walked out and got into his car without looking back at the only home he'd ever known.

One

The tiny snick of sound made by someone turning the knob on the door would have gone unnoticed, had Cody been asleep. However, the airless primitive room directly over a raucous Mexican cantina did not lend itself to quiet, restful sleep. Cody had decided a couple of hours ago that his choice of a room would never meet the AAA requirements for travel accommodations.

He had been lying there for what seemed to be hours, gazing at the pattern of light on the wall reflected from the gaudy neon sign flickering its liquid-refreshment advertisement outside his window. He had been thinking about his recent visit with his family and questioning his sanity in choosing this particular life-style. He could have been at home in his very comfortable bed, instead of lying there on the lumpy mattress unable to sleep.

When he discovered that there was no lock on the door, he had considered placing the only chair in the room beneath the doorknob. After a moment of deliberation, he had decided against the idea. He had doubted that anyone would be foolish enough to bother him.

Obviously, he had miscalculated.

No doubt whoever was intruding either had the wrong room or was under the erroneous impression he would be easy pickin's for a thief because he was *un americano*.

Cody reached beneath his pillow and slid the pistol hidden there into the palm of his hand. Making no sound, he eased from the narrow bed and in a few silent strides stood directly behind the door.

The cheap bulb in the hallway cast a thin stripe of light on the wooden floor when the door eased open. Cody watched the laser-thin line widen, then suddenly disappear as a body noiselessly stepped into the room.

Before the door closed completely, he got a glimpse of a feminine profile and long hair. In a low growl directly behind the unknown woman, he said, "I don't care what you're selling, sweetheart, I'm not buying. Now get out."

She gasped and whirled around to face him. "Cody?" she whispered urgently.

The flickering light coming through the dirty glass window caught the side of the woman's face as she turned, but even without the sight of her face he would have recognized her by the sound of her voice. Carina Ramirez was the only woman he knew who spoke his name in quite that way, her husky voice invariably accenting the second syllable of his name.

Shock ran through his body, with the realization that Carina was in his room. His mind whirled with all the reasons why this person could not possibly be here. The young girl would be the last female to enter a man's room at this late hour—or any other hour, for that matter.

The word he muttered was short and unprintable. Despite all logic, Cody had to accept the physical evidence before him. She was actually standing there.

What the hell was she doing there? She had absolutely no business being anywhere around him.

Then he suddenly realized that he was standing there buck naked. Her eyes would soon be adjusting to the light. His friend Alfonso's extremely sheltered little sister was about to receive the shock of her life.

Fury and embarrassment swept over him in equal parts. Thrust into a situation not of his own making, Cody felt the helplessness of not being the one in control. He didn't like the feeling at all.

He reached for his worn jeans and growled, "What in the hell are you doing here, Carina?" He kept his voice low, even though he didn't expect anyone outside the room to be able to hear over the racket of loud music and strident voices coming from downstairs.

He tugged the tight jeans up over his muscled calves and thighs, keeping his back to her in an effort to save them both from further embarrassment.

"Cody, I had to come," she said from behind him, her voice trembling. "I had to w-warn you." Her voice broke on the last words.

He glanced over his shoulder, while he zipped his jeans. Turning to face her, he frowned and asked, "Warn me? What about?"

The light fell across her face for a moment. In the wash of bright colors dancing over her, he could see her expressive black eyes staring up at him, imploring him to believe her. "Some men, they are coming here. They plan to kill you."

Whatever was going on, Cody knew that Carina fully believed what she was saying. Her wide eyes, trembling lips and tense body eloquently spoke to him.

He took her gently by the arm and led her to the bed. Easing her down to sit beside him, he took her hand in an attempt to comfort her. She was little more than a child, after all. Whatever had pushed her into braving her brother's wrath and risking her reputation had to be taken seriously, regardless of his doubts. Perhaps she had misunderstood what she had heard. After all, why would anyone be plotting against him in her hearing?

She lived with her brother, a wealthy landowner whose hacienda sprawled in the foothills of the Sierra Madres, an hour's drive from Monterrey. Cody and Alfonso had known each other for the four years since Cody began to work on this side of the border. They had become friends.

Surely, no one at the hacienda would have reason to want Cody dead.

He reached out and pushed a wave of hair away from her face. Cody could well understand Alfonso's protectiveness of his young sister. There was no denying Carina's delicate beauty... from the midnight black of her hair, which rippled down her back like a waterfall, to her mysteriously dark eyes, which slanted ever so slightly above her high cheekbones. Even in the poor light, her fair skin glowed like the finest of porcelain.

Alfonso was justifiably proud of his beautiful, young sister and guarded her from the men who visited him, Cody included.

In the four years he had known Alfonso and his sister, Cody had never been alone with her. Looking at her now, he could not ignore the fact that she had grown into an exotic beauty. However, the innocence in her shining eyes reflected how untouched she was by the world around her.

Placing her small hand between his large ones, he searched for and managed to find a soothing tone, before he said, "Tell me about these men, *chula*. Do you know them? Have you seen them before?"

The light from the street lamps betrayed the color in her cheeks at his term of endearment, but her gaze never wavered.

"I was in my room. I had left the doors to my balcony open for air. I hadn't gone to sleep yet when I heard voices coming from the courtyard below. Curious to see who was there, I tiptoed over to the door and peered out. They were directly beneath my bedroom balcony so that I couldn't see them, but I heard some of their conversation quite clearly. The room was dark and they had no way of knowing that I was there." Her voice shook so that he had to concentrate in order to understand her.

He slipped his arm around her and pulled her closer in an effort to comfort her. "Don't be afraid, little one. It's okay, now. Take a couple of deep breaths . . . that's it. Relax. You managed to find me. Nobody is going to hurt either one of us. Not if I can help it." He ran a soothing hand down her back and hugged her close to his chest. "Can you tell me what these men were saying?"

She pushed back and looked at him with an imploring expression. "But Cody, we must hurry. I don't know how much time we have before they show up here. They were planning to come tonight."

He glanced around the room with frustration. He could deal with a couple of men coming after him much easier than he could deal with having Alfonso's sister sitting there trying to save him. If someone *was* plotting to take him out, he had to get her out of there. But he needed more information. Fast.

"Carina," he said, placing his hands on her shoulders. "Listen to me. I need to know what you overheard. Tell me."

She drew in some air, emitting a soft sob, before she answered. "I didn't recognize their voices. There were two of them, one with a deep voice. I had difficulty hearing *everything* he said. But I recognized your name and began to listen. They were talking about you being in their way and that it was time to get rid of you."

A bolt of adrenaline shot through him. Perhaps his work was finally netting some results. He must be getting close to some drug sources who were feeling the pressure, but the last place he had expected to find them was at the home of Alfonso Ramirez.

"Did they say why they had to get rid of me?"

"Only that they didn't trust you. They think you work for the government." She sounded puzzled and uncertain.

What had he done to arouse suspicion? Perhaps nothing. All Americans south of the border were watched by those in the drug trade. There was no reason for him to believe that his cover had been blown.

There could also be other explanations to what she had overheard.

"Did they mention any other names that you can recall?"

She was silent for a moment. He assumed she was trying to remember when she finally lifted her head and he saw the agonized expression on her face. "Only one. Alfonso."

"Alfonso! Did you warn him, as well?"

Tears trickled down her cheeks and she shook her head. In a tone so low it was almost inaudible, she whispered, "No. I am afraid that it is Alfonso who told them to get rid of you."

Cody stiffened. This latest shock, coming as it did after a series of them, almost caused him to reel. He and Alfonso had never discussed Cody's reasons for spending so much time in Mexico. They had accepted each other at face value, finding they had a great deal in common. After running a check on Alfonso, Cody had been relieved to find that Alfonso had a clean record and was a very respected businessman who was above suspicion. Over the years, he had begun to trust Alfonso more and more.

How could he have so completely misjudged a person? Had Alfonso been secretly watching and laughing at Cody's naive acceptance of him? Was Alfonso the man whose organization he had been seeking all this time?

The irony of Alfonso's sister coming to warn him was not lost on Cody. The question was, what was he going to do with her now?

"How did you get here, *chula?*" He knew the small village was at least ten miles from the hacienda, much too far for her to have walked. A car leaving the hacienda would have been noticed immediately. Had she placed herself in danger by her foolhardy need to warn him?

"I slipped out of the house as soon as I could after the men left the courtyard. I knew I had to warn you, but I didn't know how. You mentioned at dinner tonight that you were staying here in the village, so I tried to think of a way to reach you without anyone in the household knowing. I didn't know what else to do, so I finally slipped away and ran to the house of Berto, my friend Angelina's brother. When I explained to him that I needed to see you tonight, he agreed to bring me to the village. Because I knew the cantina had the only rooms available for visitors I came up the back steps, looking for you. I peeked into the other two rooms, but they were empty." Her smile was filled with relief when she added, "I was very happy to finally find you."

The thought of what could have happened to her if those other two rooms hadn't been empty, the thought of the many risks she had been taking on his behalf, infuriated him and he exploded with barely suppressed anger.

"For hell's sake, Carina. Couldn't you have just sent me word of what you overheard? You should never have taken the risk of slipping out this late at night. Any number of unspeakable things could have happened to you."

Even the thought of some of them unnerved him.

A silent pause was interrupted by the sound of breaking glass, and boisterous laughter drifted up to them from the cantina below. The music never faltered. They faced each other.

She nodded slightly and said with a quiet dignity, "Berto offered to give you a message, but I didn't want him to know my suspicions. He thinks I am enamored of you—" her cheeks filled with color "—and I allowed him to believe it. Besides, I didn't think you would accept such a message from a stranger. I knew that I must come myself."

Cody could no longer stay seated. He stood up and began to pace. "All right," he growled, running his hand through his hair. "Fine." He reached the end of the room and turned, pacing toward her. "I can follow your reasoning, even if I'm appalled by the chances you took." He sat down beside her and reached for his boots. While he was pulling them on, he said, "I want you to know that I appreciate what you've done for me." He grabbed his shirt and slid his arms inside the long sleeves. "Now, then, you let me handle the situation from here. Run back downstairs and have your friend Berto take you home. Hopefully, nobody has discovered that you're not tucked into bed sound asleep." He reached out to her and she took his hand, allowing him to pull her to her feet.

He turned away and headed toward the door. He had his hand on the doorknob when she spoke behind him.

"I told Berto not to wait—that I would visit with you and that you would see that I got back home safely."

Cody felt another shock run through him. This was obviously his night for calamity in various shapes and forms. What the hell was he going to do with her? How could she have blithely planned to warn him, then expect him to see to her safety, as well? Slowly he turned to face her, unable to hide his reaction to this

latest tidbit of unwelcome information. Before he
could find the necessary words to tell her exactly what
he thought of her behavior, she nodded toward the
door and, in the calmest voice he had heard from her
since she first arrived, said, "We can't go that way. It
is too dangerous."

Ignoring the fact that she had obviously decided
that they were a team working together, he glanced
around the room. Other than the two windows over-
looking the street, there was only a small opening with
a grill cover placed high on the side wall for ventilation. He walked over to the windows and looked out.
There was a great deal of activity along the street, despite the late hour. Even if he felt like playing Tarzan
to Carina's Jane by swinging out of one of the windows and lowering both of them to the ground, they
couldn't possibly escape that way without attracting
attention.

He looked back at her, frustrated by her newfound
mood of quiet dignity. "What do you suggest we do,
then?" he asked irritably.

She pointed to the small ventilation opening.

Cody knew for a fact that a steep ravine ran along-
side the building on that side. There was a good
twenty-foot drop. "Forget it. We'd break our necks."

"No! Please listen, Cody. Berto and I discussed it
when we first arrived. No one would think to watch
this side of the building. He found a ladder in the back
and we propped it against the wall between the two
rooms on this side. Luckily, you weren't in the room
on the opposite wall. We would have had to come up
with something else."

"And how did you manage to explain to Berto our
possible need for a ladder? Does he think this is some

kind of an elopement?'' Cody could feel himself losing control of some of his frustrated anger and clenched his teeth.

"Not exactly. I just told him that I didn't want to be caught in your room, so we thought about another way out, just in case.''

Cody sighed. Save him from overimaginative children. He couldn't allow her to stampede him into doing something silly. Hell, he didn't need to run. He wanted to find out more about these two characters. The only way he could do that would be to hang around and form a welcoming committee of one.

He fished into the pocket of his jeans and brought out his car keys. "Look, *chula,* I don't need an escape route. If someone's looking for me, I want them to find me. I want to know who's after me and exactly what they want.''

He walked over and took her hand, placing the keys in her palm and curling her fingers around them. "Here. I want you to take my car and go home. Use some discretion about where you leave it, so I won't be accused of sneaking back to the hacienda for some obscure reason. Maybe we can save your reputation, yet. Perhaps it would be a good idea if you did slip out another way. There's no reason to take any more chances than we need to, at this point.''

"Please, Cody. You must leave as well. I don't want anything to happen to you. If you won't come, then I will stay here, too. Between the two of us, maybe we can—''

"Dammit, Carina! You're being ridiculous. What possible use do you think—''

He paused in his tirade, listening. The noise from downstairs still reverberated throughout the building, but he had just heard a protesting squeak of the aging floor outside his doorway, signaling that he was about to receive more company.

He realized that his time had run out. He could stand there and debate the issue with this wisp of a girl, and possibly get both of them killed, or he could go along with her escape plan. Since someone was already outside the door, he had little choice but to accept her alternative route.

Grabbing the chair, he quickly—and with a minimum of sound—wedged the back beneath the doorknob, then took her hand and pulled her across the room. Lifting her above him, he waited while she removed the grill, then scrambled through the opening. He checked to make sure his pistol was in the waistband of his jeans at the small of his back, while she lowered herself out of sight.

Grabbing the sill of the opening he pulled himself up, then through the narrow opening. He had a tougher time getting his larger body through the small area than Carina had. He was forced to place one shoulder through at a time, then pretend to be a contortionist, in order to swing his legs out toward the ladder.

There was barely enough light to create shadows, and Cody felt a momentary relief when his foot brushed against the ladder. He lowered himself, finding a couple of rungs where he could brace himself.

None too soon. He heard the doorknob rattle as he quickly climbed down the ladder.

When he reached the bottom he glanced around, peering into the gloom. He felt a small hand grab his and tug him away from the wall.

The area on this side of the cantina had been allowed to return to nature. The steep slopes and heavy underbrush obviously had discouraged the citizens of the small settlement from cleaning the area out of a civic need to beautify the town's landscape. Cody had cause to feel grateful at that moment for the townspeople's lack of pride, as he and Carina moved through the heavy brush deeper into the ravine and away from the noisy cantina. The brush was vicious to move through, tearing at their clothing, but Cody didn't lessen his pace. Now that his course of action had been set, he was determined to get Carina away from the area until he felt it was safe to circle to where he had hidden his car just outside the town, then get her home.

He continued to follow the twists and turns of the ravine, but the going was slow without light. Carina had prudently dressed in black slacks and sweater, so that only her face was a faint blur in the shadows.

She hadn't made a sound since they had left the room. He was amazed at her bravery. Everything had happened so fast. His brain was still sorting and filing away the information he had received in the past few minutes. He didn't doubt that Carina had heard something definite enough for her to risk dire consequences in her effort to warn him.

He just wished that she had gotten a glimpse of the men. Since she had not recognized their voices, there was a good chance they were not part of the group that had gathered for dinner at the hacienda earlier that evening.

The thought that Alfonso might be behind this threat shook him. Could his instincts have been so wrong about the man? During the years he had worked in this area, he had uncovered several pockets of drug smuggling and seen them stopped. He felt useful and he felt that his time was well spent.

Alfonso Ramirez and his home had offered a haven of sorts, a place for Cody to visit in order to rest and relax. Alfonso had been insistent earlier that night that Cody stay at the hacienda, but Cody had planned to get an early start to Monterrey and hadn't wanted to disturb the household by his early departure.

Had his refusal to stay forced Alfonso into a change of plans? Could his friend be plotting to have him killed? The thought sickened him. He would not have given the matter a moment's consideration if Carina had not felt that he was in danger and that the danger came from Alfonso.

What must that have done to her? Cody continued to be amazed that she had chosen to contact him. He still couldn't fathom her reasons for doing so. Although he had seen her often during the years, and had treated her with the kindly indulgence of an uncle to a young girl, Cody could not recall anything he might have said or done that would justify her possible betrayal of her brother's plans in order to save Cody.

Her courageous actions baffled him.

The one thing he was absolutely sure of was that he had to get her back to the hacienda before she was discovered missing. Whatever else happened, he must protect her from her own impulsive behavior.

When he finally paused for breath, Cody discovered that they were only a few yards from a dirt road. Still holding Carina's hand in a firm clasp, he led her through the remaining underbrush out onto the road.

As though celebrating their escape, the moon came from behind a low-hanging cloud and flooded the surrounding landscape with a silvery radiance that filled Cody with relief. With light and a decent road to follow, he would be able to find his car in no time.

He turned to Carina in time to see a shadow separate itself from a nearby clump of trees and grab Carina.

"What the—?" Cody felt a burst of pain at the back of his head. The fading moonlight was the last thing he remembered.

Two

Carina felt an arm snake around her throat at the same time she saw a shadowy figure strike Cody on the back of his head. She watched in horror as Cody fell in a crumpled heap at her feet. Without conscious thought she struggled to get away from whoever held her in an effort to see if Cody was badly hurt.

Surely they hadn't made good their intent to kill him!

She fought with desperation—kicking, biting and clawing at the arm around her throat. She caused enough damage to her captor that he let out a yell and released her, cursing. Ignoring the two men, she ran to where Cody lay and fell to her knees beside him.

"Cody? Are you all right? Oh, Cody," she whispered feeling the knot already forming at the base of his skull. She pressed her cheek against his, feeling his warmth and hearing his quiet breathing. She closed her eyes in relief, holding him.

One of the men grabbed her by the arm and yanked her to her feet. Carina winced, but refused to acknowledge the pain she felt from his grip. She realized, as she glanced up at the tall, shadowy man, that he was the one who had hit Cody. In Spanish, he began to tell off his companion for not hanging on to her. The man immediately answered with equal spirit in his own defense.

From what she could gather, these two men had been told to watch the ravine as a possible escape route. They had not really expected Cody to get this far. They certainly had not expected to find him with a woman.

The ensuing argument revolved around what to do with her. From listening to them, she discovered that they had explicit instructions not to harm Cody if they should catch him. She found that remark reassuring, although the knot on his head and his unconscious status revealed that at least one of the men had his own interpretation of harm.

Carina could feel her heart pounding in her chest. She couldn't remember another time in her life when she had been so frightened, not even when she had slipped away from the hacienda earlier and had hiked through the darkness to Berto's home. Obviously she had not overreacted to what she had heard. Cody was in grave danger, despite everything she could do.

Were these men part of the same group she had heard plotting? Was it possible there was more than one group looking for him?

Ever since she had heard Alfonso's name mentioned Carina had fought her pain and panic at the possibility that her brother could have ordered the death of their friend.

She still could not grasp what was happening. How could her brother possibly betray his friend? Cody had become a familiar figure in her life. She had been such a child the first time he had come to their home— barely sixteen, she knew that she looked more like twelve at the time. Despite her lack of stature, he had treated her as an adult—with teasing respect and a gentle dignity that had endeared him to her, causing her to look forward to the periodic visits of the tall and very attractive Texan.

When she had overheard those men earlier tonight, she had known immediately that Cody had to be warned. Since she couldn't be certain that Alfonso wasn't part of the conspiracy, she had to find a way to contact Cody, herself.

Now she was a part of whatever was going on. Her warning had not helped him at all.

The men had finally stopped arguing. They took what Carina assumed to be handkerchiefs and tied her hands and feet together, warning her that if she gave them any trouble they would knock her out as well. At least she knew Cody was alive. She would just have to wait and watch for a way to help him.

She cried out in shocked surprise when they covered her eyes. One of the men slapped her, hard, across the mouth, causing her lower lip to bleed. Helplessly she ran her tongue across her lip, feeling the puffiness forming. One of the men picked her up and carried her a brief distance, then placed her on a ridged surface that felt like the flooring of a pickup truck. Jostled by movement beside her she knew that Cody lay nearby. A truck engine started, causing a vibration in the surface beneath her cheek. The painful joltings of the truck bed told Carina they were moving, but she had no idea where they were going, or in what direction.

In an attempt to distract herself during the uncomfortable ride, Carina forced herself to think about more pleasant things. Her thoughts turned to Cody.

She would never forget the first time she saw him. She and her mother had been sitting in the courtyard of the hacienda when her brother had appeared in the doorway with a blond giant of a man who wore a heart-stopping grin on his handsome face.

"I can't believe this, Alfonso," she heard him saying. "Your place is practically a duplicate of the Big House on the Circle C Ranch. Of course, our family has added a couple of additions since the original hacienda, but if I didn't know better, I would think I was stepping into my mother's courtyard. Even the plants and flowers look familiar."

"I would like you to meet my mother and my sister, Carina," Alfonso said, motioning for the man to come toward them.

To Carina, he looked like a sun god, with the light glinting on his blond hair and tanned skin. He had taken her hand in his, and said, "I'm very pleased to meet you, Miss Ramirez." He glanced at Alfonso. "I envy you having a sister, something I've missed in my life." He went on to speak to her mother, and they had chatted, but Carina didn't pay much attention to the words. Instead, she focused on the sound of his deep voice, and watched the play of his smile across his lips.

A few years before she had read a magazine article about the Texas Callaways. The article had displayed several pictures of the three brothers. Even then, her eyes had been drawn to the blondest, the one with the winsome smile. She and her friend Angelina had giggled about how handsome the men were. She had never thought she would be able to meet one of them. Cody Callaway was even better-looking in person. As charming as he looked in the magazine, no picture could do justice to the magnetism that surrounded him, making him appear larger than life.

"I insist that you stay for dinner, Cody," Alfonso had said, and Carina had added her silent pleas.

"Well, if it wouldn't be too much trouble—" he drawled in reply, and Alfonso laughed.

"In this household, there is more than enough for everyone."

He had stayed and Carina had sat across from him at dinner, enthralled with his anecdotes, shy but pleased that he noticed her and teased her from time to time.

Over the years, Cody had added color and excitement to her otherwise boring routine of school and home life. Even after she had finished her schooling and returned to the hacienda permanently, she had looked forward to his visits, eager to listen to his stories and glimpse a freedom she had never experienced.

Looking back she could better understand the crush she had developed—not only on the man, but on all that he represented. Cody was different from anyone else in her life. She found him fascinating.

He had never encouraged her in any way to see him as anything but a family friend. Eventually the infatuation had turned into a comfortable friendship.

She had put her childish dreams away once she knew what she wanted in her life. She wanted a taste of the freedom that had once fascinated her in Cody. She would always be grateful to Cody for giving her a glimpse of such a life.

However, she couldn't ignore what she had heard tonight, couldn't take the chance that by not getting word to Cody she might be contributing to his death.

She was not sorry that she had attempted to warn him. The only thing Carina regretted was that the warning had come too late to save him.

The first thing Cody saw when he managed to open his eyes were a pair of black eyes watching him worriedly. He blinked and groaned, the pain from the back of his head insistently making itself known.

"Cody? Are you all right?"

He closed his eyes again. That voice. He thought he had dreamed that Carina had come to his room, but she was still here. What the hell was she doing, hovering? Didn't she know he had the daddy of all hangovers? How could he entertain some innocent little—no, wait a minute. He hadn't been drinking. He and Carina had—

Cody opened his eyes again, trying to figure out where he was, where *they* were. He was lying on his back. With a sudden flash of memory he reached beneath him, but he knew before he felt along his waistband that his pistol was gone.

"Where are we?" he muttered in a gravelly voice. Damn, that was an original line if he had ever heard one. The universal question of all time, he supposed, pushing himself up on his elbows, then edging his legs over the side of the bed.

"Don't try to move, Cody. You may have a concussion. You need to lie still." Carina placed her hands upon his shoulders.

He ignored her efforts to restrain him, and forced himself to sit up and look around. "Forget my head. I need to know where we are."

As far as he could tell, they were in a one-room cabin. The sound of heavy rain falling against tin made him look up at the roof. From the obvious age of the place, they should be thankful the roof didn't leak.

The last thing he remembered was seeing the moon and thinking they were through the worst of it. Then one of the shadows had moved and—

He glanced around at Carina who was watching him with concern. "Are you all right?" he asked.

She nodded.

"Can you tell me how we got here?"

"Two men brought us. They tied me up and blindfolded me. I have no idea where we are. We seemed to have traveled for hours." She, too, glanced up at the roof. "I think we were very fortunate to arrive before the rain started. We were in the back of an open pickup."

Cody eased himself off the bed and gingerly made his way to one of the shuttered windows. "Something tells me we weren't left alone here. Where are the men who brought us?"

"I haven't seen them. When the rain started, I heard them talking about leaving before they got stranded. I think we must be in an isolated part of the mountains. I peeked out the door earlier, but couldn't see anything at all."

Cody rubbed the back of his head, feeling the large knot there, and cursed under his breath. He pulled open the shutter over the window and attempted to peer out, but the night and rain blocked his view.

He turned. "So why didn't they kill me? They had every opportunity."

"I don't know. I heard them discussing that they were only to guard against your escaping through the underbrush. I think they were more surprised than we were to see them."

"I wish to hell I knew what's going on...who's behind this."

"Perhaps we should leave here before someone comes back," Carina offered.

He had already thought of that. Had he been alone, Cody would have acted on the idea, but he couldn't go off and leave Carina, and he didn't dare drag her out into the elements without a clue to where they were or how far they were from help.

"Let's wait until morning. Maybe the weather will have cleared some by then." He prowled around the room, noting the antique wood-burning cookstove, which Carina must have stoked. There was a kettle of water steaming on top, while a small fire danced in the fireplace nearby.

He walked over to the sink and grabbed the pump handle there. After a couple of pumps, water came gushing forth. A row of canned goods sat on a shelf above the sink.

"At least we won't starve," he muttered.

"Are you hungry?"

He filled a glass with water and drank before answering. "No, just thirsty." He turned and looked at

Carina, who had risen and was standing beside the only bed in the room. "Have you had any sleep?"

She shook her head. "I couldn't. I was afraid you might need something and I wouldn't hear you."

"Then you'd better try to get some rest. We may have a strenuous walk ahead of us when light comes."

She nodded, obviously seeing the sense in his suggestion. He watched as she stretched out on the bed where he had been a few minutes earlier. With a little sigh she closed her eyes, obviously exhausted. He walked over to her and picked up the folded blanket at the foot of the bed. He spread it over her, then turned away.

"Okay, Callaway," he muttered to himself. "You're always so good about getting yourself out of tight places. What do you intend to do now?"

He would be much happier if he had some idea where they were. How long had he been unconscious? He rubbed the back of his head. Whoever had slugged him knew what he was doing. He hadn't broken skin, but had inflicted damage.

Cody paced between the fireplace and the window, watching for any sign of light, artificial or from the sun. Once in a while he would glance at the sleeping girl. Had he been alone he would have handled all this so differently. He wouldn't think twice about getting away from here and finding a place to watch for anyone returning. If the weather let up, he would suggest that they leave the cabin, rather than sitting there waiting for their abductors to return.

The rain continued to beat down on the tin roof, creating a monotonous drumming. Eventually the sky lightened to a heavy gray, but the visibility was scarcely increased through the rain and haze. By mid-morning the wind had picked up, causing the small cabin to shudder in the sudden blasts.

Cody went outside at first light and explored the area surrounding the cabin. Bluffs rose directly behind the cabin. He eventually found the trail with the recent tire tracks that marked their entry into the valley-like canyon. There was no sign that anyone else had been here in a long time.

Obviously they couldn't depend on a transit system to get them out of there. The cabin blended so well into the bluffs that it disappeared from view within a few hundred yards. Even the smoke from the chimney was camouflaged by the gray stone behind it.

By the time he returned to the cabin, he was soaked and more than a little disheartened.

Without saying anything to him when he burst inside the cabin and slammed the door, Carina filled a large mug with coffee and silently handed the steaming cup to him.

"Thanks," he said gruffly, reaching for the hot liquid.

"You need to get out of those clothes, Cody," she said softly, handing him a worn but clean towel and the quilt from the bed. She turned away and busied herself at the stove.

He knew she was right, but he didn't like the idea of stripping down. However, his choices were limited. With a muttered curse he sat down and pulled off his boots, then shucked out of his pants and unbuttoned his sodden shirt.

After briskly rubbing the towel over his chilled body he gratefully wrapped the quilt around him, draping one end over his shoulder, and sat down in front of the fireplace.

"Did you get some idea where we were?" she asked, filling a plate with hot food and handing it to him.

"Not a clue," he muttered. He placed the mug on the table and began to eat. When he was finished, he glanced up at her. "Aren't you going to eat?"

"I already have, while you were out." She turned away and walked over to the window. "Do you think we should attempt to find our way out of here?"

"Not in this weather. We're somewhere in the mountains, and they become treacherous after a hard rain. There's too much danger from flash flooding or softened trails that suddenly break away."

She turned back and met his eyes for the first time since she had awakened. "I've made things worse for you, haven't I?"

He glanced up from his contemplation of the fire dancing in the fireplace. "In what way?"

"Those men would not have been able to harm you. You would have heard them coming, as you did me, and been prepared. I've placed you in more danger, rather than helping you."

"You did what you felt you had to do, *chula*. I know you meant well, but a young girl like you shouldn't be exposed to this kind of thing—" he waved his hand to encompass the primitive cabin.

For the first time since they had been together, he saw a glint of amusement in her black eyes. "I don't consider twenty particularly young, Cody. Perhaps where you come—"

"Twenty!" Carefully setting the hot coffee down on the table, Cody came to his feet. "What are you talking about? You can't be twenty."

She raised her right hand and did a quick cross over her heart with her left one. "I swear I am. How old did you think I was?"

He shrugged and turned away, feeling the heat of embarrassment steal across his face. "I dunno. Fourteen or fifteen, maybe. Just a kid."

She laughed, a light tinkling sound that Cody had always found to be infectious. "I may be young, Cody, but not *that* young!"

He forced himself to look at her again, this time with eyes that assessed what he saw, rather than what he remembered. Suddenly he felt old, much older than the ten years that made up the difference between them. Regardless of her age, Carina appeared to be untouched by life and some of the tough knowledge that can rip away the innocence of a young person.

He winced at the reminder.

"What's wrong?"

"I'm sure that Alfonso has missed you by now."

"Oh! That's probably true. Perhaps he will be looking for me," she started excitedly. Then, as though remembering the rest, she said, "What if he's the one who had you brought here?"

"Actually, that thought has crossed my mind. Is it possible that we're on part of his land?"

"I don't know. I haven't been able to tell much from the doorway and the window. I know that I've never seen this place before."

He rearranged his clothing in front of the fire, pleased at how quickly they were drying. If he did have to greet his captors, he would much prefer wearing more than his skivvies.

To preserve the little modesty he had managed to hang on to, Cody readjusted his quilt and sat back down. Motioning to the other chair, he said, "Maybe you'd better sit down and tell me a little more about yourself. I seem to have missed something over the years—such as your growing up."

Carina sat down and folded her hands. "What would you like to know?"

"I thought you were a schoolgirl, obviously. Start there."

She cocked her head to the side, as though thinking. "Well, I did attend a parochial boarding school in Monterrey, until I graduated three years ago. Then, I attended the university in Mexico City for two years. At the moment Alfonso and I are at odds. I've had an offer to attend a university in the states. He wants me to stay here and get married."

"Married!" Cody repeated before he could stop himself. All right, there was no reason for her not to consider the matter at twenty, he supposed. "Is that what you want?"

She shook her head vehemently. "No way. I've been drawn to working with a special-education training, to help children with speech impediments to talk. I'm very interested in this and would like to make working with children a career. But Alfonso is so old-fashioned. He wants me safely married." She made a face. "He's already found me a husband. Hah! Someone that *he* approves of, of course."

"Do you know the man?"

"Yes. He's someone I've known for years, but I have absolutely no desire to marry him! He's too old, for one thing."

Cody decided not to ask her what her idea of too old was, for fear she might think he was ready for retirement, himself. "I see."

"The problem with Alfonso is that he is too protective of me. He always has been. He treats me like a child. He doesn't trust my judgment."

"I wonder why," Cody drawled.

"You see? You do think I should not have tried to warn you."

"That hardly matters at this point, now, does it? What matters is what Alfonso will do when he finds you. If he *is* behind all of this, he'll see your attempt to warn me as a betrayal. If he isn't behind it, he'll feel that your reputation has been compromised. Either way, your brother is not going to be pleased with either one of us over this little deal."

"How can you joke when your life could be in danger?"

"I'm not joking, and it's both of our lives, sweetheart. Do you think they're going to allow you to walk away from here, just because you're a woman?"

"I suppose not. Perhaps it's because I thought Alfonso was behind this that I have been feeling safer. He would never do anything to harm me. This I know."

"I thought I knew your brother pretty well, *chula,* but now I'm not certain of anything. I suppose the best thing that could happen would be if—"

He never got to complete that sentence. The door burst open behind them and three men stepped into the room with guns pointing at them. Cody slowly came to his feet and turned, deliberately placing himself between the gunman and Carina. The quilt settled around his waist and effectively hobbled his movements.

Well, hell. Once more he had been caught without his pants on. This was getting to be a habit he didn't much care for.

The first man inside the door said, "Get your hands over your head, Callaway, and keep them there." The slight movement was all the quilt needed to slither to the floor, leaving him standing there in his briefs.

Three

"So you are the famous Cody Callaway," drawled the man standing before him. The other two closed the door and leaned against the wall, smirking.

"I'm afraid you've got the advantage," Cody replied in a lazy tone. "I don't believe we've ever met."

"Ah, yes. I definitely have the advantage now, don't I?" He nodded toward Carina. "Who is this woman? I wasn't expecting to find you with anyone last night."

Cody shrugged.

"As for my name, I doubt it means anything to you. I am Enrique Rodriguez. Kiki, to my friends."

Cody fought to maintain a passive expression, but he could not control the sinking sensation he felt in his chest. Here was the man he had been searching for, but this was the not the way he wanted to confront him.

"Are you responsible for our being here?" Cody asked.

Kiki nodded, smiling. "This was not the original plan, of course. But my men did very well. They have brought you here so that I may deal with you, myself. I have long wanted to meet one of the sons of Grant Callaway, face-to-face."

"Did you know my father?" Cody asked in an attempt to buy some time for them. He shifted slightly, his body now behind the table. If he could keep Kiki talking long enough to better shield Carina, perhaps she would have a chance to get through the next few minutes.

As soon as he had heard the name of their abductor Cody knew he was a dead man. From everything he had learned about him, Cody knew that resentment had twisted Enrique Rodriguez's mind as well as his entire perspective on life. There would be no reasoning with him.

"Oh, yes. I knew the high-and-mighty Grant Callaway. I went to him with a business proposition years ago. I explained how he owed me and my family. With the money he could have given me, I would have been able to make a success of my business, but he turned me down." Kiki wiped the back of his hand across his mouth. "But he paid for his arrogance," he growled. "I made certain of that. Just as I intend to make every one of you Callaways pay. You're all the scum of the earth."

So his suspicions had been correct. This man was responsible for the death of his parents. He had discovered the truth, but there was no way to let his brothers know...unless he could convince Rodriguez to let Carina go.

Without losing eye contact Cody shrugged his shoulders in a nonchalant manner, and said, "So? There's no reason to involve my girlfriend. She has nothing to do with any of this."

Kiki spit. "She's trash. Otherwise she would have nothing to do with such slime as you."

A slight movement at one of the windows caught Cody's eye. Someone was out there. Was it friend or foe? At this point it didn't matter. He had to try something. He rammed his hip against the table, forcing it onto its side, then grabbed Carina as the table toppled and shoved her behind it. The loud discharge of pistols filled the room, but he didn't allow the distraction to stop him from making a dive for Kiki's knees. The force of his body knocked Rodriguez off balance. The pistol in his hand went flying.

Cody straightened, bringing his right fist up with all his strength, and connected with the man's jaw.

Rodriguez folded like an overextended accordion being released. Dimly Cody had been aware of glass shattering and the door bursting open once more. Now he spun around in time to see the other two men with their hands over their heads.

He smiled at the newcomers, who were holding guns pointed toward the intruders. "Hey, Freddie. Am I ever glad to see you!"

Three more men came inside, one wearing a uniform. "I understand you are having some problems here?"

Cody nodded. "As a matter of fact, I have reason to believe this man—" he nodded to Enrique Rodriguez who lay unconscious on the floor "—is responsible for years of harassment and possible murder with regard to my family. I've been down here gathering evidence on this man and trying to locate him. Obviously he found me first." He rubbed his stinging fists, then looked down at his hand, surprised to see that his knuckles were bleeding and beginning to swell.

"Then you wish to press charges against him?"

"You bet. For kidnapping and attempted murder. If Carina hadn't—" Carina! He spun around and saw her huddled against the table, her head buried, her shoulders shaking.

He strode to the overturned table and knelt down beside her. "Are you all right?"

She looked up and saw him. With a look of relief, she threw her arms around him. "Oh, Cody! I thought they had killed you. There was so much noise and shouting. I saw you move toward that man and—" She shuddered, burying her head into his shoulder.

He awkwardly patted her on the back. "You're okay, baby. I believe the cavalry got here in time."

He continued to kneel there beside her, while the authorities took Enrique's men away. In an effort to calm her, Cody lifted Carina in his arms and walked over to the bed. When he attempted to lay her down, she clung to him with a sob. He sank down on the bed and continued to hold her, this time in his lap, while he stroked her hair and murmured soothingly to her.

Looking back on the scene later, Cody could understand Alfonso's first impression when Carina's brother stepped through the cabin door. But his understanding came later, much later.

When he got his first glimpse of Alfonso, he smiled with relief. "Your timing couldn't have been better, Alfonso," he said.

Alfonso trod silently across the floor, his expression murderous. "Get some clothes on, you son-of-a—'' He paused, obviously in an effort to gain some control over himself. "We'll talk about this later."

Only then did Cody remember that he was clad only in his briefs and that Carina was snuggled up to his bare chest as though she had found a permanent home.

"Uh, Alfonso," he began, reaching behind his neck and insistently removing Carina's trembling arms. "I know what this must look like to you, but if you'll just let me explain—"

"I fully intend to hear every one of your explanations, Cody," the man replied in a deadly tone. "But for the moment, I want you to let go of my sister."

Cody spread his arms wide, knowing that this was no time to begin an argument. He had never seen Alfonso in such a rage. "Carina, honey," he murmured. "Let me get some clothes on, okay?"

He knew he had done something else wrong when Alfonso's face darkened even more. Carina lifted her head, her eyes red from weeping, her cheeks moist. "Alfonso?" she whispered, her eyes filled with dread. "Alfonso, please don't hurt him. I couldn't bear it if something happened to Cody."

Cody realized that Carina hadn't seen how Alfonso's men had come to their rescue. She must think that Alfonso had been in charge of their kidnapping, after all.

Wanting to reassure her that her brother had not in fact plotted to have him killed, Cody began, "Carina, you—"

Alfonso interrupted him. "Shut up, Cody. Just... shut...up." He made a quick motion with his head toward the fireplace where Cody's clothes were spread.

Cody lifted Carina from his lap and put her on the bed, then headed for his clothes. The other men had all left the cabin, so that only the three of them remained.

Cody wasted no time pulling on his clothes, which were thankfully dry by this time. He stamped each foot to make sure his boots were solidly on, then glanced across the cabin. Alfonso was talking to Carina in a voice too low for Cody to hear. No doubt he was reassuring her about his part in the recent events.

"How did you know where to find us?" Cody asked the first question that crossed his mind.

Alfonso reluctantly turned away from Carina and looked at Cody. "As soon as I discovered that Carina wasn't at the hacienda I had men scouring the area, looking for leads. Luckily we made early contact with Roberto Escobedo, whose sister is a friend of Carina's, and he explained his part in helping her to meet you. That's when I doubled my forces in an effort to find you."

"Well, actually, I don't think he understood what—" Cody began, but Alfonso waved him to silence.

"Once we arrived at the cantina, the owner told us about some men who had been looking for you. By that time, some of my other men had located and questioned the two who had transported you in the truck. They very graciously gave us directions to this cabin."

"Then you know that we were forced to come here," Cody pointed out in a carefully reasonable tone.

"Oh, yes. I'm very much aware that Carina had expected to return to the hacienda before anyone had discovered that she was not there."

"She overheard—"

"Come," Alfonso interrupted. "Let's get these fires out and leave this place." He touched Carina's cheek. "I want to get Carina home."

Cody heard the control Alfonso was still using to restrain his temper and decided not to push the matter at the moment. Given time to calm down, Alfonso would no doubt be more receptive to explanations.

Or so Cody hoped.

"Look, Alfonso," Cody said hours later, facing his friend across the massive desk in Alfonso's study. "I know you're upset with me. I know what you must be thinking, but if you would just let me—"

"I am thinking that given my preference I would much prefer to kill you, rather than have to deal with you at all. But since that would not repair the damage done to my sister's innocence or to her reputation, I have reluctantly given up the idea."

"Dammit, Alfonso, there is nothing wrong with Carina's reputation, and as for her innocence... that's what I'm trying to explain—"

"Perhaps in Texas a young woman can be coaxed into meeting a man without her family caring, but not here in Mexico!" Alfonso came to his feet, as though unable to sit still for another moment. "What sickens me is how much trust I placed in you. I befriended you. I did everything in my power to assist you in hunting down this man Rodriguez. And how do you repay this assistance, this trust?" he asked, slamming his hand flat on the desk. "By seducing my sister!"

Cody leaped from his chair. "I did not seduce your sister!" he shouted, leaning both arms on the desk and glaring at Alfonso. "How many times do I have to tell you that? She overheard some men plotting to kill me and came to warn me."

Alfonso made a sound of contempt. "How ridiculous. How could she hear someone plotting such a thing in my house?"

"I don't know. But she did."

"If Carina had heard such a thing, she would have come to me immediately with the information."

"Not if she thought you were behind the plot."

For the next few moments Cody was afraid Alfonso was going to have a stroke. His color changed with alarming suddenness and he stood there staring at Cody, his mouth moving silently.

Cody started around the desk, but Alfonso backed away, taking in several deep breaths of air. "Don't you dare try to make me think my sister considers me a killer, because I will never, ever believe such a thing. You are lower than a snake, to suggest the idea in an effort to drive a wedge between us." Alfonso strode over to the French doors that opened onto the courtyard of his home. Opening one, he stood with his back to Cody while he stared out at the colorful profusion of the garden.

Cody heard the steady trickle of water from the fountain in the courtyard. He, too, took the moment to get his emotions under control. He wanted to handle this explosive situation with as much detachment as possible.

Without turning around, Alfonso said, "There is no use in your making up lies, Cody. Roberto told me that Carina came to him and begged him to give her a ride to where you were staying. She made it clear to him that she wanted to see you again that night, and that if he didn't take her, she would go alone. She made no mention to him of any plot." Alfonso turned and pinned Cody with a cold stare. "I find it offensive enough that you should betray my family by making an assignation with my sister, but to convince her to come to you late at night—to place her in such unnecessary danger—was reprehensible." Slowly he paced to where Cody stood. "You are not a man. You are worse than a seducer of innocent women. You are a liar and a coward. I hope you rot in hell for what you have done to Carina and to our family."

Cody could not remember a time when he had needed to exert so much self-control over his urge to smash his fist in another man's face. He had never allowed a man to speak to him in such an offensive manner. Never. To have those words come from his friend infuriated him. Alfonso knew better. He knew Cody too well to believe all the things he was calling him. Yet because of his rage over what had happened, he was throwing away their friendship, declaring a state of perpetual enmity between them.

Cody stood there, clenching and unclenching his fists, gnawing on the inside of his cheek, and searched for the wisdom to handle this volatile situation. There was absolutely no doubt left in his mind that Alfonso had meant what he said—he would have preferred killing Cody to speaking to him.

The fact remained that he had chosen not to kill him. Why? Cody knew the answer. Because of Carina.

"What do you want from me, Alfonso?" Cody asked in a level tone.

"What I want and what I insist upon are two different things. If I had my way, I would make certain you never came south of the river again. But I can't. Too many people know."

"Know what?"

"That Carina was with you when you were kidnapped, that the two of you spent the night together in a secluded mountain cabin."

"Alfonso, nothing happened between us. You've got to believe that. *Nothing!* I respect Carina. I respect her very much. I would never, *ever,* take advantage of her."

"Perhaps you did not have the opportunity this time. Of this, I have no way of knowing. Just as I have no way of knowing how often she has slipped away to be with you in the past. This time, through unusual circumstances, the two of you were caught before she could return home."

"Alfonso! Will you listen to me? I am not your sister's seducer. Never, at any time, have I seen her without a family member being present."

Alfonso clasped his hands behind his back and rocked back and forth from his heels to his toes. "Until last night when she suddenly decided to throw away twenty years of training, tradition and maidenly virtue to visit you in your room after midnight. Is that what you wish me to believe?"

Cody sighed, and ran his hand through his hair in frustration. "I told you why she came."

"I know what you told me. Having those men kidnap you no doubt gave you an opportunity to place the blame on Rodriguez. What you want me to believe is that some of the people working for me might be in Rodriguez's pay. What you want me to believe is that my sister, who loves me and who knows that I worship her, thinks I would plot to have one of my friends killed. Do you really think of me as that stupid, to believe such an idiotic story? Please do not insult my intelligence, Callaway. Even my patience has its limits."

Cody threw up his hands. "I give up. Believe what you want to believe. I'm certainly not going to be able to change your mind. I can see that now." He turned and started toward the door that opened into the hallway.

"Where do you think you're going?"

Cody was so angry he wanted to hit something, and knew that he had to get out of there before that "something" became "somebody." The situation was strained enough without his taking a swing at Alfonso. He met Alfonso's gaze with a determined one of his own. *Believe what you like,* he wanted to say. *I no longer care.*

"I'm wasting my time here. I can see that. If I can get a ride to my car, I'm going to check with the authorities to see what they are doing about Enrique Rodriguez. Then I'm going to call my brother and tell him what's happened."

"You are contacting your family?"

Cody heard the sarcasm but couldn't figure out what had provoked it. "That's right. Do you have a problem with the idea?"

Alfonso smiled, but the smile was far from pleasant. "Not at all. I suggest you invite them to your wedding. We will make the affair as public as possible. There will be no shoddiness regarding this matter to reflect on Carina. There is no reason for her to suffer any more embarrassment than has already taken place."

Cody gave his head a quick shake, thinking his hearing was playing up on him. "What did you say?" he asked, staring at Alfonso in disbelief.

"I believe that you heard me quite well. I have been planning a party for this coming Friday for several weeks now. We will formally announce your engagement at that time. You may invite your family, if you wish. We will discuss the date for the wedding over the weekend."

Cody considered himself a reasonable man. He seldom allowed his emotions to control him, but this was one time that he didn't trust himself to speak right away.

Marriage? Him? Hah! Marriage was the very last thing he intended to experience. Hadn't he made that clear to everyone who knew him?

"Now wait just a damn minute here," he said, moving back toward the center of the room where Alfonso stood, still clasping his hands behind his back. "I'm sorry that Carina got mixed up in all this mess with Rodriguez. I certainly never intended to get innocent people involved. I mean, I have nothing against your sister or anything, Alfonso. She's a real sweet little gal and all that, but I'm not the marrying kind, you see. I like my freedom, and my whole life-style is geared to my being on my own. She'd be miserable married to someone like me and you know it. You can't just go around arranging other people's lives like that. Marriage is a serious business. Nothing to be taken lightly, Alfonso."

The room filled with silence after Cody stopped speaking. Alfonso continued to watch Cody as if he were some unsavory specimen that he was having trouble identifying. When he finally spoke, he said, "Carina is the joy of my life. I remember when she was born. Our father died of a heart attack while Mother was carrying Carina. The first time I held her in my arms I promised to protect her, to be the father she would never know. I have done the very best I could to keep that vow." He turned away and walked behind the desk once more. He sat down, reached for one of his cigars, rolled it between his fingers, trimmed it, then carefully lit it before inhaling. Cody recognized the insult of Alfonso's not offering him a cigar.

After taking a few puffs, Alfonso looked up at Cody once again. "There is only one reason my sister would have risked so much for you, Callaway. She must fancy herself in love with you. I don't know how you were able to coax her to your side, but the facts are there and neither of you deny them. The intimacy between you is more than evident—any doubt I might have had was erased when I walked into that cabin and found the two of you together—and you undressed. I would have staked my life on the fact that my sister had never been alone with a man in her entire life." He sighed. "I would have died, obviously. Whatever your magic, you have seduced my sister. The evidence is overwhelmingly against you. If you are any kind of a man at all, you will do what you must to make amends."

"I—" Cody paused, collecting his thoughts. "But, you—" Once again he came to a halt, rubbing his hand over his mouth. "I mean, Carina doesn't really—" Cody stumbled to a complete halt, suddenly aware of the giant hole that had sprung into being before him. Here was the true test of his worth. He knew that he was an honorable man. He knew that he was an honest man. He had always taken his integrity for granted.

Now he was faced with some very disagreeable choices. He did not want to hurt Carina in any way. After all, she had risked her life, as well as her reputation, in an attempt to warn him of danger last night. The fact that he had not needed her protective gesture was moot at this point.

What had happened last night could not be undone. The question was, what did he intend to do about the situation now?

He wished that he could talk to Cole and Cameron. They had always advised him well in the past. He didn't want to make any hasty decisions that would have irrevocable consequences in his life, not to mention in the lives of others.

"Alfonso," Cody began once again, trying to find the words to explain what he felt. "I think we're both too emotional at the moment to be making rational decisions. I think if we give the matter time, give *ourselves* time to cool off and to think with a little more clarity, we can come up with some alternate solutions that would be more beneficial for everyone. Carina mentioned that she hoped to continue her schooling. Perhaps we could wait until after—"

"Absolutely not. Do you think I would allow her to run the risk of being unwed and pregnant—"

"Pregnant! Now wait just a damned minute here, Ramirez. I keep telling you over and over. I have not touched Carina. Not in any way. There is no way she could possibly be pregnant!"

"You forget that I saw the two of you together, with my very own eyes. She was clinging to you, obviously comfortable being around you, while you sat there wearing no clothes. Do not talk to me about how you haven't touched her. I know better.''

"Well, she sure as hell isn't going to get pregnant from having my arms around her.''

"I never thought she would. But you had several hours of privacy that are unaccounted for. A close intimacy could have evolved by the time I arrived.''

Cody felt as if he were caught up in some senseless nightmare where logic and reason were being used against him. He felt like a defendant on the stand who was guilty unless he could prove his innocence.

"Why don't you talk to Carina about this, Alfonso? She'll tell you that nothing happened between us. She'll—''

"She will say whatever you wish her to say, I'm sure of that. She obviously feels obligated to protect you.''

"So you think we are both liars, is that it?''

"I think that Carina loves you. Because she loves you, she will do whatever is necessary to protect you. As for you . . . I believe I've made my opinion of you quite clear.''

"You certainly have.'' Cody couldn't believe what was happening. He struggled to find words to convey his shock. "I'm surprised you would want someone like me to marry your precious sister.''

"I want my sister to be happy. She has made her choice. Like it or not, I must accept it.''

"Even though you're giving me no choice.''

Alfonso removed the cigar from his mouth and curled his lip.

"You made your choice when you spent the night with my sister. Now I expect you to face the consequences. That is, if you're man enough to do so.''

Cody had been through a rough twenty-four hours. He had done his best to deal with the startling and tumultuous events with honor. He had done everything he knew how to do to hang on to his control, but his detachment was at an end and his temper flared.

"All right, Alfonso. If you are so damned desperate to get your sister married off, then so be it." He strode to the door, pausing only long enough to look over his shoulder and say, "And yes, you can count on the fact that my family will be here on Friday night to witness the fiasco of your engagement announcement."

Four

As soon as Carina opened her eyes, she remembered that today was a very special day. She lay there for a few moments, luxuriating in the quietness that surrounded her. She knew the silence wouldn't last long. By noon their guests who had a fair distance to travel would be arriving to attend Alfonso's party.

The party had been planned for weeks. She and her mother had insisted that there be a special celebration for Alfonso's fortieth birthday. After much discussion, he had finally agreed, but only if the purpose of the party were kept private between family members.

Carina didn't care, so long as they set this time aside to honor her brother. Thank God Alfonso had known nothing of the plot against Cody. Not that she could get him to discuss the matter with her. In fact, he had refused to discuss the subject the few times she had seen him this week. He would only explain that the men behind the plot were all in jail, where they would no doubt remain. She was sorry that she ever thought Alfonso could have been involved.

He confirmed that Cody would be attending the party tonight, which was wonderful news. She hadn't had an opportunity to speak with Cody since they had been rescued from that cabin in the mountains.

She'd had nightmares the first couple of nights after the incident—dreams of guns going off, people grabbing her—she had been afraid to fall asleep at night. She had wanted to talk about it, first with Alfonso or perhaps Cody, but neither had been available. Gradually the harsh memories subsided and her sleep was made easier because of her busy days.

Everything was ready—all of the extra bedrooms had been cleaned and filled with fresh flowers, awaiting their occupants. Even the buildings surrounding the hacienda had been cleaned. She had noticed yesterday that Alfonso had some of the workers cleaning the small chapel that had been built many years ago. She supposed their visitors would be fascinated with its history and would be going through the various outbuildings, but was surprised that Alfonso had given the matter much thought. When she had peeked inside, she had been surprised to see some of the women polishing and cleaning the altar and mopping the stone floors, while the men scrubbed the stained-glass windows and oiled the wooden pews.

Puzzled by the activity, she wondered if Alfonso intended to hold a special mass in the historic building in honor of his birthday.

Whatever his intentions, she reminded herself, she needed to stop daydreaming. There were still last-minute preparations that needed her attention.

By the time she returned to her room to prepare for the dinner that would accommodate their out-of-town guests, Carina was more than ready for a brief rest. The tension and excitement of the household staff and occupants had continued to build, as more and more friends and relatives gathered at the hacienda. Once she saw that her mother and brother were there to handle greetings and to direct people to their rooms, she slipped away.

Her one disappointment of the day was that Cody had not arrived by the time she returned to her room. She almost asked Alfonso if he had heard from Cody, but at the last minute decided not to mention the Texan to her brother. There was something that Alfonso wasn't telling her where Cody was concerned. Whenever she mentioned Cody's name, Alfonso brushed her remarks aside with impatience and changed the subject. They must have had words, but if so, Alfonso wasn't going to discuss the matter with her.

She could only hope that Cody hadn't changed his mind about attending the party. She had never properly thanked him for being so kind to her during that horrible night.

As soon as she reached her room, Carina slipped out of her clothes and walked into her bathroom. After filling the oversize bathtub with bubbles and scented water, she stepped into its depths and sank down with a sigh, the soothing liquid swirling around her body. She could feel the tension begin to leave the muscles in her neck, shoulders and spine.

She closed her eyes and thought about the dress her brother had surprised her with earlier in the day.

Never had she seen a more beautiful gown. It was like nothing she had ever had before. This dress was ivory satin decorated with cream-colored lace. The neckline came to the edge of her shoulders, then dipped slightly into a V in front, leaving her neck and upper shoulders bare.

The dress narrowed at the waist, then billowed out into a multitude of tiny satin ruffles edged in lace until it reached the floor. Several petticoats came with it, including one with a hoop in the hem. She would need help getting dressed, her mother had pointed out, and promised to be up later after Carina had had time to rest.

She closed her eyes, resting her head along the rim of the tub. Her thoughts were never far from Cody Callaway. She kept thinking about what he had looked like without his clothes, how he had felt as she had clung to him. She could almost smell the slight scent of his warm body, feel his smooth skin stretched across the muscled plane of his chest. She squirmed with her memories. Of course she was uncomfortable with her thoughts. She had never been in a man's company like that before. She knew it was wicked of her to dwell on the memories, but she was fascinated all the same.

She wondered what it would feel like to be kissed by Cody Callaway. She smiled to herself, allowing her thoughts to drift and whirl around her much like the water that encircled her body.

"Carina? Where are you?"

Carina came awake with a jerk and realized that her bathwater had grown cold. "In here, Mama," she replied, hastily rising and reaching for a towel. Her eye caught the movement of her reflection in the mirror and she paused for a moment, staring at her familiar image. Slowly she wrapped the towel around herself without taking her eyes off the mirror and stepped out of the tub.

Her hair had come loose from the pins she had used to keep the heavy mass piled on her head, so that one long curl fell across her shoulder and curled around her breast.

Oh, if only she were taller! She still looked like a child, standing there wide-eyed. She wanted to be voluptuous and seductive, someone who would catch the sophisticated eye of Cody Callaway and make him aware of her as a woman.

Instead, she looked slender and unsure of herself — much too inexperienced for a man such as Cody.

"You must hurry, Carina, or we will both be late for dinner."

"Yes, Mama," she responded, continuing to dry herself.

When she walked back into the bedroom, she found her underwear and petticoats already spread across the bed. After slipping them on, she raised her arms while her mother dropped the satin dress over her head. Carina slid her hands into the armholes and helped tug the dress in place. By the time her mother fastened the small buttons along her spine and straightened her hem, Carina's eyes had grown wide in wonderment. The creamy ivory was the same shade of color as her own skin. She rubbed her fingertips across the edge of the neckline that rested along her shoulders, feeling as though some fairy godmother had waved her wand and turned her into a princess.

"Ah, Carina," her mother whispered in awe. "Never have I seen you look more beautiful."

She reached for her mother's hand. "How will I ever be able to thank Alfonso? I can't believe this, can you?"

"Well, we must arrange your hair and get downstairs before he sends someone looking for us," her mother said in a practical tone. After Carina sat down in front of her vanity table, her mother pulled Carina's hair high on her head, then allowed it to cascade down her neck and shoulders in a froth of curls.

The dinner bell chimed as they began their descent down the winding stairs. Carina had stuck a gardenia behind her ear while her mother had fastened a double strand of pearls around her neck. She felt as if she were living out a fairy tale—Cinderella had arrived at the ball.

"Ah, Carina," Alfonso said, coming to wait for her at the bottom of the stairs. A sheen of moisture in his eyes made them glisten in the light from the massive chandelier overhead. "You look enchanting, my love. Utterly enchanting." He took her hand and raised it to his lips. When he raised his head, he glanced to the side of the hallway and said, "Don't you agree, Cody?"

Carina hadn't seen Cody standing in the shadowed doorway of Alfonso's study. Now he stepped forward. She tightened her grip on the rail for balance and stared down at him, her heart racing. He was here!

He wore a tuxedo of Spanish design. The red cummerbund accented his trim waistline, the short jacket enhanced the width of his shoulders and the snug trousers molded his muscular legs. She could not read anything from his expression. He stared at her as though he had never seen her before.

Forcing herself to continue down the last few steps, Carina kept her gaze on him. Why didn't he smile? Why did his mouth appear almost grim?

"Come, Mama," Alfonso said, holding out his arm, "you are just in time for me to escort you to dinner. Our other guests are all assembled." He turned and stared down the hallway. Cody silently held out his arm to Carina.

Tentatively she placed her fingers on his arm, feeling the tensed muscles beneath the finely woven cloth of his jacket.

"Hello, Cody," she said, wishing her voice didn't sound so strained. "I wasn't sure if you would be here tonight."

"Weren't you?" He followed Alfonso down the hallway. Carina slightly lifted the hem of her gown and kept pace with him. She peeked a glance at him, then dropped her eyes. His jaw could be made from a slab of granite, it looked so hard. After that first look at her, he had stared straight ahead.

"I looked for you after we got back from the mountains last week, but Alfonso said you had business to attend to."

"Yes."

"Did it have something to do with that horrible man who had us kidnapped?"

"Partly. I went to Texas to see my brothers, as well."

"Oh."

They arrived in the dining room. Alfonso was already seating his mother at one end of the table. Cody pulled out the first chair at the other end for Carina, next to where Alfonso would be sitting, then sat down beside her.

"Carina, I would like you to meet my brother Cole and his wife, Allison," he nodded to the couple beside him. "And my brother Cameron and his wife, Janine." He nodded to the couple opposite them.

"Oh, Cody! How wonderful. I had no idea your family would be here tonight." She smiled at the two couples. "I am so very pleased to meet you. What a wonderful surprise."

Both men nodded without speaking or smiling, looking as solemn as Cody. The women smiled. The dark-haired one, Allison, said, "Your dress is lovely, Carina." The red-haired one added, "I was thinking the same thing. You look radiant."

Carina could feel her cheeks heating. "Thank you," she murmured, just as Alfonso sank into his chair at the head of the table and signaled for dinner to begin.

"Have you been introduced to the Callaways?" Alfonso asked Carina.

"Cody just introduced us. Why didn't you tell me they were coming?"

Before Alfonso could answer, Cody said, "You mean you didn't know?"

"Not who was coming, just that we had two more bedrooms to prepare for overnight guests." She smiled at the other couples. "I can't tell you how happy I am to meet you like this. As busy as you all must be, I'm amazed you found the time to be here."

"Oh, we wouldn't have missed this party for the world," Cole drawled. "Right, Cameron?" He lifted his wineglass and made a toasting gesture to his brother.

"Absolutely," Cameron replied, lifting his glass in response and taking a swallow.

"Very funny," Cody muttered.

By the time dinner was over and the dinner guests began to mingle with the others who had arrived for the dance, Carina felt as though she had been cast in a play without being given a script. There was a definite undercurrent going on during the various courses of dinner. Although the surface conversation between her brother and the Callaway brothers was all very polite, there seemed to be some very pointed remarks that she could not understand in the slightest.

She excused herself as soon as dinner was over, feeling the need to take something for the beginning of a throbbing headache. By the time she made her way back to the massive room, which had been cleared of furniture for the four-piece band and dancing, the place was filled with laughing guests pursuing various pleasures. Several couples were out on the dance floor, others had gathered around a table set up as a bar, still others stood in groups chatting.

Carina paused at the wide archway into the room and looked around, pleased to see that everything seemed to be flowing smoothly. The canapé trays were receiving admiring attention and those working out of the kitchen were efficiently restocking.

"Quite a party."

Carina gave a start, not having seen the tall, solid man come up behind her.

"Oh! Hello. You're Cole, aren't you?"

Cole grinned. "That's right. You've got a good memory."

"Not really. It's just that I've heard so much about you . . . and Cameron . . . that it wasn't difficult to figure out which one was which."

"I had no idea Cody was such a chatterbox."

Carina chuckled at his tone of voice. "You must remember that we have known each other for some time. I've always been interested in his family... and the ranch... and he's been patient enough to answer all my questions, regardless of their impertinence."

All the while she was talking, Cole seemed to study her, his eyes piercing. His lazy smile belied the serious expression of his gaze.

"Would you care to dance?" he asked rather abruptly.

Carina glanced toward the crowded dance floor, then smiled. "I would like that very much."

Cole led her around the room with an air of command, drawing her out. "I was surprised to be introduced to so many people who were your sisters and brothers," he said, after nodding to one of her brothers and his wife as they passed by. "For some reason I had the idea that you and Alfonso were the only ones in the family."

"Oh, no. There are six of us, altogether. Alfonso is the oldest. I am the youngest. I'm the only one left at home, you see."

"So I gathered. Your other sisters and brothers are married?"

She sighed. "Yes. Which has been Alfonso's argument whenever I talk about going on with my schooling. He thinks I should be content to marry and care for a family, as Rosie and Conchita have done."

"You disagree?" He raised one of his brows.

"Someday I hope to marry, of course. But not now. There is so much more to do in life," she said, smiling. "But now, I'm getting off on one of my tangents, as Alfonso calls them, when we are supposed to be relaxing and enjoying ourselves."

"How could I not be enjoying myself, dancing with a beautiful woman like you?" Cole responded.

She hated the blush that she knew flooded her face. She knew he was only being polite, but she had never been comfortable with compliments.

"Mind if I cut in, bro?"

Carina could feel her body react to the sound of Cody's voice. Cole glanced down at her, then responded with flattering reluctance. "Well, if you insist, but I figure there are lots of gals around you could enjoy dancing with."

"Then you shouldn't have any trouble finding one," Cody replied. He slipped a very possessive arm around Carina's waist and pulled her to him. Ignoring his brother's amused chuckle, Cody spun her in a series of fast turns that caused her to lose her breath.

When she regained her balance and some air she discovered that he had danced her through the wide French doors out into the courtyard. Although a few couples lingered out there, the light was dim and there was a greater sense of seclusion.

"You and Cole seemed to find a great deal to talk about in there," he said, watching her with a narrow gaze.

"I like your brother. He's friendly and very kind."

"Cole? Hah. He's about as friendly and kind as a barracuda. At least most of the time. I guess he's always been a sucker for a beautiful woman, though."

"Cody?"

"Yes?"

"What's wrong? You've been in a strange mood all evening. Your brother was just being polite. Why does that make you angry?"

"It doesn't. I'm glad you had a chance to visit with him." He slid his hand up her back, then down, as though restless.

"Are you upset with me?" She gazed into his stormy eyes, wishing he would tell her why he was so disturbed.

"Now why should I be upset with you?" he drawled.

She was quiet for several moments, thinking. "I'm not sure. Are you still angry because I came to your room that night last week?"

"I think it's a little late in the day to go over that, wouldn't you say?"

"Then you *are*. I wondered if that's why you left without talking to me again."

"I wasn't in the mood to talk to anybody when I left here."

"Aren't you glad that man was arrested?"

"Very."

"So it worked out all right in the end, don't you think?"

He stared at her for a long moment. "You think so?"

She looked at him, confused by his manner. "Don't you?"

He slid his hand up to between her shoulder blades, then made a couple of rapid turns before settling both arms behind her, leaving her little choice other than to rest her hands on his chest.

"Uh, Cody, I don't think Alfonso would like it very much if he saw you holding me in such a manner."

He muttered something beneath his breath that sounded like "tough," but Carina knew she must have misunderstood him.

With his chin resting lightly on top of her head, he asked, "What has Alfonso told you about tonight, Carina?"

Carina could scarcely think. All she could do at the moment was feel Cody's presence. She hadn't realized how much she had missed the feel of his arms around her until he held her close once again. She could feel the steady pounding of his heart beneath her fingertips, hear his soft breathing, smell the special scent that made up the essence of who he was. How could she possibly concentrate on his question? Something about Alfonso.

She moved her head so that she could see his face. "Tonight? Well, only the closest family knows, but today is Alfonso's birthday, which is why we are celebrating."

"That's all?"

Puzzled at his insistence, she said, "What more could there be?"

He muttered something under his breath that she was almost glad she couldn't decipher. "He told me he would handle it, and like an idiot, I believed him."

"Handle what? Is this about my being with you that night?"

"Yes."

She'd never heard the word more clipped.

"Well, actually, I haven't seen much of Alfonso this week. Every time I attempted to explain why I was there and what I tried to do he waved my explanations aside, as though he knew all about it. I assumed the two of you discussed the matter and he understood what had happened."

The band completed the song they were playing. Instead of going into another one immediately, as they had been doing all evening, there was a drumroll and a harmonious blast of trumpets, causing everyone to take notice.

Cody turned so that they both faced the end of the room, where Alfonso joined the bandleader on the dais. He stepped in front of the microphone.

"I hope everyone is having a good time this evening," Alfonso began with a smile. The room erupted in clapping and cheering. He waited for everyone to become quiet before he continued. "We have a very happy announcement to make this evening, something of a surprise that I hope you all will enjoy. We always feel blessed when our friends and our family come together in celebration. Therefore, we decided to take this opportunity to share another event."

He looked out over the sea of faces, his gaze meeting Carina's. He held out his hand. "Carina, would you please join me?"

She froze, wondering what he was doing. She had assumed that he had decided to tell his guests about his birthday, but there was no reason for her to be there, was there?

The people stepped aside, leaving a wide aisle for her to move through the crowd. She glanced up at Cody, but could read nothing in his expression. With as much grace as possible, she left the courtyard and walked to the end of the room.

Alfonso took her hand, then turned her to face the waiting crowd. "There are times when it is difficult for a brother to admit that his sister has grown-up." Carina nibbled on her bottom lip and attempted to hang on to her smile, reminding herself that no one had actually died of embarrassment. "As many of you know, Carina recently finished her studies at the university in Mexico City."

Oh, my gosh! He had changed his mind! He was going to allow her to go on with her education! And he had chosen to surprise her with the news tonight. She almost grabbed him in an exuberant hug as she heard him say, "Now she is ready to move on to the next stage of her life."

She could feel the bubble of excitement climb within her. She could hardly refrain from laughing out loud. So this was the reason for the very special dress. He was willing to honor her wishes and allow her to make her own choices.

"It is with great pleasure and an enormous amount of pride that I invite you to witness the next part of our festivities, the wedding of my very precious sister, Carina, to Cody Callaway."

The unexpected news stunned the room, but Carina could not fully appreciate their reaction. She had to deal with her own. She stared in horror at the man who still stood beside the fountain in the courtyard watching the scene being played out inside.

Scattered clapping accompanied by the buzz of excited voices filled the air. Carina saw Cole and Cameron move toward Cody as though in protection.

If this was some kind of bizarre joke, there was no one laughing.

Alfonso's voice sounded once more over the microphone, drowning out the noise and her swirling, chaotic thoughts. "May I present the bridegroom, Mr. Cody Callaway?"

Despite everything she could do, Carina's knees buckled. She would have fallen if Alfonso hadn't grabbed her around the waist with one hand while he held out his other hand to the man threading his way through the milling crowd, his brothers no more than a step behind him.

Somehow she managed to focus on Cody's face...on his eyes, which were snapping with fire and suppressed emotion. Nimbly he leaped up on the dais beside her, his arm snaking around her waist, lifting her away from Alfonso as he pulled her tightly against his side.

"Are you all right?" he asked in low tone.

"All right? Of course not. How could I—" she turned and looked at Alfonso "—How could he—"

Meanwhile, the fun-filled crowd applauded Cody's possessiveness and cheered him on.

Still at the microphone, Alfonso said, "Now, then, if you will follow our bride and groom across the way to the family chapel, we will continue with the night's festivities."

The crowd began to move away, leaving Alfonso standing there with Cody and Carina. Cole and Cameron were nearby.

"This wasn't the agreement and you know it," Cody said as the noise abated.

"Care to explain what's going on?" Cole asked from a few feet away.

Alfonso faced Cody, then allowed his gaze to take in the possessive way Cody held Carina to him. "I would say that it is obvious, wouldn't you? We're about to witness a wedding."

"But, Alfonso," Carina began, "this can't be. Why, Cody and I, we aren't—" She looked at Cody's stern countenance and shuddered, "We can't do this. Why are you—"

"Because he has the upper hand and intends to use it," Cody said. He glanced at his brothers. "I should have figured on something like this happening, but I had hoped he would have second thoughts about the whole situation after having a few days to reconsider." He stepped off the dais, then turned and lifted Carina down.

"You knew he planned to do this?" she asked Cody, shocked.

"Not exactly. I agreed to his announcing our engagement tonight. He's the one who decided to make a circus out of the event."

"Our engagement! But Cody, how could you agree to such a thing? We are not engaged. We have never discussed it. How can—"

"That's enough!" Alfonso said. "Whether you discussed the matter or not, you most certainly should have before you chose to slip out to see him whenever you could. It sickens me to think that my sister would stoop to such behavior."

"Alfonso! What are you saying? There is nothing between Cody and me. Nothing! How can you do this? I thought you loved me. I thought you were going to allow me to continue with school. Why would you—"

"Come! We're wasting time. Our guests are waiting for us in the chapel."

"I don't care! You can't just—"

"Carina," Cody said quietly, "I appreciate the fact that you are no more enthused about this little merger than I am, but the fact is that you're wasting your breath. Your brother isn't the least bit interested in hearing the truth. He's found you a wealthy husband and isn't about to let go." He glanced over at Cole with a half smile. "He kinda reminds ya of a terrier who won't let go once he's caught something, doesn't he?"

Cole didn't return the smile. "Cody, are you going to let this character get away with this? He has no legal right at all. You know that."

Cody looked at Carina for a long time without saying anything, before he turned back to Cole. "The way I figure it is, she's a hell of a lot better off with me than with him. At least I'll listen to her, which is more than he seems to be capable of doing."

"No!" Carina said. "I can't let you do this, Cody. This is not at all what you want."

Cody stared at Alfonso, who met his gaze without flinching. "Let's just say I like the alternatives even less, all right?" He glanced at his brothers. "Well, it looks like I've got me a couple of best men here. Let's get over to that chapel and get this little matter taken care of."

Without a backward glance, the three men walked off, leaving Carina standing in the empty ballroom with Alfonso. Slowly she turned and faced her brother.

"I have loved you all of my life. You have been the father I never had—you've been my friend, my confidant. But if you make me marry Cody Callaway under these conditions, I will never forgive you, do you understand me?"

"Carina, listen to me—"

"No. You listen to me. You and Cody must have discussed all of this last week, but you did not consider consulting me about my feelings or my desires. You went ahead and planned the whole thing around me."

"I assumed you would lie to protect him."

"I don't have to lie. Cody Callaway has never been anything but a complete gentleman with me. For you to use what I did—without Cody's knowledge or permission—against him is reprehensible. If you have any feelings for me at all, Alfonso, you will go over there and explain to those people that there has been a mistake and that there is not going to be a wedding."

She waited, knowing that she was fighting for her very existence. She didn't have to wait long.

"I cannot do that, Carina. Surely you can see that. It is too late."

"It is *not* too late. Only your pride will suffer, Alfonso. But if you force me to go through with it, not only my life but Cody's will be permanently marred."

"Nonsense. You are much too dramatic, little one. It is just because of the surprise that you are so upset. But I felt it would be better so. Now, come. We must not keep them waiting any longer."

Carina felt as though a blast of arctic wind had entered the room, swirling around her until she was numb with shock and despair.

Cody was waiting to marry her in the chapel, but only because her brother had forced him into agreement. How could she face the man she admired, knowing that she was being forced upon him?

Alfonso took her arm and began to lead her out of the room, across the garden area and into the chapel, where Cody waited beside the altar with the priest.

There was no place for her to run, no person who could help her. Once again Carina felt the sense of helplessness that had oftentimes swept over her when she disagreed with Alfonso's choices for her.

She scarcely noticed the candlelight and flowers that had transformed the chapel into a fairyland. All she could see was Cody, his gaze trained on her face, waiting to see what she would do.

All of her dreams and her fantasies of her future exploded into bleakness as she heard the small organ begin the slow music that would accompany her down the aisle.

This wasn't what she had thought her wedding day would be. How could she have imagined herself marrying a cold-eyed man, without notice, without a trace of courtship, being urged down the aisle by her brother who had betrayed her on the most profound level?

The deep inner trembling that had begun at the first wave of surprise and horror had increased until her entire body shook. Only Alfonso's firm grip on her elbow kept her from falling. With the inexorable movement reminiscent of a nightmare, Carina moved ever closer to the altar and the men waiting there.

She focused her attention on Cody, whose face seemed to have softened in the light from the multitude of candles. His lips turned up at the corners in a slight smile of self-mockery that she found endearing, given the circumstances.

When she reached his side, Cody took her hand and turned toward the gentle man who would perform the rites of matrimony. Cody's hand was warm as it enveloped her icy one. He squeezed her hand slightly, as though for reassurance, and for the first time since Alfonso had made his startling announcement, Carina found herself taking a slow, deep breath of air.

This was Cody. Whatever happened in the future, she knew that she could trust him. At the moment, that trust was the only thing she had to cling to.

She was going to be his wife.

Five

Cody allowed the traditional words of the age-old ceremony to calm and soothe him while he held Carina's hand in his.

He knew that his brothers were just behind him, in the front row reserved for his family. He was thankful for their presence.

Earlier in the week, he had discussed Alfonso's demands with Cole and Cameron, looking for a better solution to the problem. Neither one of them had thought he should allow himself to be pushed into an engagement, even a short one.

Normally he would have agreed with them, but they didn't know Carina. She didn't deserve the embarrassment of being jilted even before the engagement had been announced. He had felt certain that once Alfonso calmed down the three of them would be able to talk about what had happened and—more important—what hadn't happened. He had hoped that Alfonso would then agree to allow the engagement to stand a few weeks before Carina ended the alliance, which would effectively save face for the family.

So he had talked his brothers into being there tonight—for moral support—having no premonition they would witness his marriage to Carina Ramirez.

During their walk to the chapel Cole and Cameron had strongly advised him to stand up to Alfonso, regardless of the repercussions. He listened and he understood their concern, but all the while he remembered the panic on Carina's face when she had realized what Alfonso had done.

He certainly didn't consider himself hero material, but he had known at that moment that he must do something. He couldn't just leave her to face all these people on her own, with a fiancé who refused to become a bridegroom.

He glanced down at the young woman beside him. Her mother and sisters had met her just inside the chapel and placed a thin veil over her head, effectively masking her features and expression when she came toward him down the aisle.

However, nothing could hide from him the pain in her eyes once she reached his side and met his gaze. She did not have to tell him that she had never intended her warning to create this situation. How could she have known that her decision that night would have so many serious and long-lasting repercussions?

Somehow they would work this out. Once married, he would be able to take her away from her brother's influence. He would take her back to the family ranch, then decide what to do. Other people had managed to salvage something from arranged marriages. There was no reason why he and Carina couldn't work out something as well.

When the ceremony concluded, Cody was encouraged to kiss his new bride. He carefully folded the veil up over her head, away from her face. Rich color rushed into her cheeks when he bent toward her, which pleased him. As pale as she had been earlier, Cody had been concerned that she was going to faint on him.

With the slightest hint of a wink and grin, he slipped his arms around her and lowered his mouth to hers. He felt her lips quiver when he first touched her, then all he was aware of was the softness, the yielding, the sweetness that was Carina.

A rush of emotion hit him. Raising his head he looked into her eyes and in a voice meant for her ears alone said, "I will always be here for you, Carina. You can count on me, no matter what happens."

Her eyes anxiously searched his and obviously found what she was seeking because she smiled, the most natural smile she had given him for some time.

"Thank you, Cody. I'm glad."

There was no more time for the exchange of confidences. They were swept to the back of the chapel in a swell of organ music and on through the gardens to the ballroom, where they were surrounded by the delighted guests, all wishing them well. Cody kept Carina tucked firmly against his side, aware that the slight trembling he had felt in her earlier had never stopped.

Once again, the small orchestra began to play. This time Carina circled the floor in the arms of her new husband, while the guests watched from the sidelines.

"Are you okay?" he asked after they made the first circuit of the dance floor and she had not spoken.

"I'm not certain," she whispered, her eyes wide. "Is this real?"

He grinned. "As real as it gets, honey."

"I don't think I can take too much more of having people stare at me."

"You don't have to. I'll take care of it."

As soon as the dance was over, Cody made their excuses and whisked her up the stairs amid a great many ribald remarks. He paused only long enough to say a few words to Cole, who nodded and gave him a pat on the shoulder.

Once upstairs, Carina led him down the hallway to her room, then paused in embarrassed confusion. "Where are you going to sleep?"

"If I know Alfonso, and I think I do, I'll bet my clothes have been transferred to your room. Care to place a small wager?"

"But surely he—" She shook her head without saying more and opened her bedroom door. Cody remained in the doorway, leaning against the doorjamb with his arms crossed. Carina hurried into her dressing room. He responded to her muffled sound of dismay with a half smile.

She came out of the dressing room with her hands clasped, a worried expression on her face. Cody straightened and stepped inside the bedroom, hooking his foot on the door and closing it behind him without glancing back.

"Don't look so upset, *chula*. You don't have anything to worry about from me, remember?"

She walked over to where he stood in the center of the room. "I will never forgive Alfonso for this. Never."

"Well, that gives us something in common right off, doesn't it?" He walked over to the French doors and opened them. Sounds of music and laughter drifted up from the courtyard.

"This is where you were the night you heard those men talking?" He didn't really care, but he thought it might help to get her mind off their present predicament, at least for a few minutes.

She hesitated, then joined him. "Yes."

"Alfonso doesn't believe there were any men. Did he tell you?"

She stared up at him in surprise. "No men? But of course there were. Why else would I have risked going to find you, if there were no men?"

He let his silence answer her.

She continued to look at him, until comprehension slowly engulfed her. "Oh, no! He couldn't have thought that— Why, he couldn't have believed that— Oh, Cody, that's why he did all of this," she said, waving her hand at her dress and at his clothes hanging in her closet.

"You got it."

"But this is terrible! How could he not have believed me when I tried to explain?"

"Because you didn't immediately go to him with your suspicions. Alfonso refuses to believe that you might have thought he could have wished me harm."

She whirled away and paced to the other side of the room. "Yes. It was very stupid of me. But I was so frightened, and I was afraid of making a mistake that might cost you your life." She spun around, her full skirt swirling. "Even so, look what has happened to you! You were forced to marry me because of my foolish behavior."

"Not forced, exactly. I mean, nobody held a gun to my head. Let's just say I was persuaded, okay?"

"But this isn't what you want!"

"It isn't what you want, either."

They stared at each other from opposite sides of the large room in a moment of shared revelation, recognizing that they were much like comrades at war with a common enemy.

Eventually Cody held out his hand and said, "You're going to need help getting out of that dress, I suspect. I have a hunch you probably don't want my assistance. Would you like to call your mother?"

"No!" Carina glanced around the room helplessly, obviously remembering when she had dressed earlier in the day. "My mother must have known about this, and yet she didn't say a word. How could she do this to me?"

"You don't know that for sure. I have a hunch Alfonso planned his little surprise very carefully in order to lessen any resistance he might have aroused."

"But my mother and sisters had my veil—"

"Your mother had just found it when I arrived at the church. Your family—all but Alfonso, of course—think that this is a true love match, that I have been secretly courting you and petitioning Alfonso for his permission for a long time. Your mother told me how delighted she was that you were going to be with me. For some reason, she seemed to believe you would be very happy being married to me." His grin was meant to be teasing, but she was too agitated to notice.

Carina reached around to the back of her dress, then made an impatient sound. "My mother can't understand my desire for more education. So she assumes that marriage would be my only goal." She walked over to him and turned around. "I would much prefer your help than to have to speak to anyone else at the moment."

He decided not to point out her less than gracious acceptance of his help. Solemnly Cody began to work on the small buttons down her back.

"I thought we might leave here fairly early in the morning and drive to the ranch. It's my home, although I'm seldom there. Now that I have a wife, I need to make some decisions about certain things."

She glanced over her shoulder. "What things?"

"Oh, just some work I've been doing. It isn't too conducive to a strong home life. Maybe it's time for me to resign and move back to the ranch on a permanent basis."

"Is that what you like to do? Ranch?"

The dress began to fall away and she grabbed it to hold the top in place. She hurried into the dressing room.

Cody sat down and pulled off his shoes, which were not as comfortable as the boots he generally wore. He stretched and flexed his toes with a sigh of relief.

"The foreman runs the ranching part of things," he replied, raising his voice slightly so that she could hear him. "I always thought that someday I might start raising horses." He ran his hand through his hair. "Who knows? Maybe now is the time to look into the idea more fully."

Carina came out of the dressing room tying the sash of her robe. Without looking at him, she walked over to the vanity and sat down. She removed the flower from her hair along with the various pins, and began to run the brush through its long length.

"Cody?"

"Hmm?"

Still without looking at him, she asked, "You're expected to sleep here with me, aren't you?"

He made no attempt to hide his amusement at her tone from her. *A guy could get a complex, if he didn't watch himself.* "That's the general idea, I think."

"You would be very embarrassed to have to find another place to spend the night, wouldn't you?"

He leaned back in his chair and in the mirror he studied the nervous and fretful young woman who refused to make eye contact with him. "I'm sure I'd survive. Is that what you want me to do?" he asked, curious to know how honest she would be with him.

She placed the brush carefully on the table in front of her before studying her hands and saying, "I don't want to do anything else that will cause you problems."

Cody took his time coming to his feet, and even more time to walk over to where Carina sat. He placed his hands on her shoulders and waited until she looked into the mirror and their gazes met.

"Carina, I know that you don't know much about men, and it's obvious that your mother didn't discuss much with you regarding marriage. So what I need to do is to let you get used to sharing your life with a male. I know that wasn't what you had planned. As far as that goes, this isn't what I had planned either, but we need to start this marriage in the way we mean to go on. Sooner or later we are going to become intimate."

He could feel her shoulders tense at his words.

Without changing the pitch of his voice, which he had chosen in a deliberate effort to soothe her, he continued. "However, we don't have to do anything about the matter tonight. We're both tired and more than a little undone by the suddenness of it all. What I suggest is that you go on to bed and try to get some sleep. I bet by morning you'll be feeling better about things, or at least will have gotten used to the situation a little more."

"But where are you going to sleep?"

"I thought I might take a long, hot shower, then maybe stretch out on the other side of that bed over there. That thing's big enough to sleep a whole bunch of people. I doubt that either one of us would know the other one was there."

He kept his eyes steady on hers, willing her to understand that he would not under any circumstances take advantage of her.

In a moment he felt her shoulders slump beneath his hands. She looked ready to drop, now that the tension had left her body. He reached down and lifted her into his arms and carried her over to the bed.

The covers had been turned back. He lowered her onto the bed, brushed her slippers off her feet and, with a deft twist of his wrist, unfastened her robe and whisked the soft garment away while he pulled the covers to her chin with his other hand.

"Get some sleep, honey. We'll talk more about this tomorrow."

He turned away and had taken only a couple of steps when he heard her say, "Cody?"

He forced himself to turn around once again, making certain that his expression remained impassive. "Yes?"

"Thank you," she whispered.

He gave her a grin and a thumbs-up sign before he walked into the bathroom and closed the door.

He leaned against the door with his eyes closed, feeling the relief of finally being alone for the first time in hours. When he opened them, he dispassionately stared at his image. Now that he didn't have to pretend, he wearily noted that his smile had long since disappeared. *You were pretty convincing, there, old buddy,* he told his image. *Almost had me fooled, and I knew how you were feeling. So the little gal's safe, is she? You're going to treat her like a sister, huh? You're going to pretend that seeing her in that filmy nightgown and robe didn't affect you, that watching her comb out her hair didn't make you want to bury your head in that glossy mass of curls. You're just a regular Sir Galahad, aren't you?*

He reached inside the shower stall and turned on the water, making certain that only cold water came pouring out. He tugged at the tie he had worn, tossing it on the marble counter before he pulled off the jacket in jerky movements. He removed the rest of his clothes, thinking about the woman lying in bed in the next room.

So he actually thought he was going to climb into that bed without blinking an eye, turn over and go to sleep as if his wife weren't lying there an arm's reach away.

His wife. Even the words set off a tingling within his body that he couldn't ignore.

Irritably he stepped under the icy deluge in an attempt to get his mind off his desires and on to what he intended to do about this fiasco of a marriage. The first thing he wanted to do was to get away from Alfonso Ramirez. The man had created enough havoc in his life for one lifetime.

Once he returned to the Circle C, he'd call his boss and discuss the situation with him. Somehow he couldn't see leaving Carina there at the ranch alone with Aunt Letty while he continued his work.

He gradually added warm water to the spray beating down on him, feeling the soothing relief on his battered body. He couldn't find the answers tonight. Perhaps there weren't any answers. Regardless of her age, Carina Ramirez Callaway was still a child in many ways. He had to give her some time and some space without taking advantage of the intimate nature of their relationship.

He had never had a tougher assignment in his life.

Carina lay there listening to the muted sound of the water and tried not to imagine what Cody must look like standing beneath the spray. She felt as if her body were on fire and she shifted restlessly on the bed, wondering what she could do to force her mind into a peaceful blankness.

He had looked so handsome, so austere, as he stood beside her in the chapel, repeating the vows in a firm voice. Nothing seemed to bother him, whether it was an attempt on his life or the sudden acquisition of a wife.

She envied him his ability to deal with life head-on without wavering. She turned her head slightly, looking at the French doors standing open across the room. She could hear the muffled sounds of conversation and laughter. Obviously everyone had enjoyed Alfonso's party and the impromptu wedding ceremony.

Carina wondered if she would wake up in the morning and discover that all of the events of this evening had been part of a dream. She might open her eyes and discover that the party was scheduled for that night. Could her subconscious possibly have dreamed that she would marry anyone, especially Cody Callaway?

Not even her subconscious could be so creative.

The bathroom door opened and Carina realized that the sound of running water had ceased several minutes before. Without moving her head she peeked over the covers and briefly saw Cody's silhouette in the doorway as he turned off the light, leaving the room in darkness except for the moonlight around the balcony.

Cody moved silently toward the French doors. Carina could feel her heart pounding as she watched him. In the brief glimpse she had been given of him, she knew that he wore only a small towel around his hips. He paused at the open doors for a few moments, watching the activities below, before he gave a barely audible sigh and quietly closed them.

Concentrating on keeping her breathing as even as possible, Carina watched as Cody moved to the other side of the bed. Her eyes reflexively closed in shock when she saw him nonchalantly drop the towel beside the bed and slide under the covers.

The bed was large enough that he was still a considerable distance from her, but all Carina could think about was the fact that Cody had come to her bed wearing nothing.

She fought to swallow without a sound, holding herself as still as possible. He had promised not to touch her, hadn't he? He had never gone back on his word, not since she had first met him.

The mattress beneath her quivered, signaling Cody's movement. She waited, not exactly certain of what she expected him to do. After a moment, the bed settled down and she risked the slight movement of her head to look in his direction. The light from the glass doors gave enough illumination for her to see him quite clearly.

He lay on his stomach with his head beneath the pillow. She could see the broad expanse of his shoulders and the way his back tapered down to where the sheet covered his narrow waist. The white sheet made a sharp contrast to his darkly tanned skin.

Carina found herself studying him with fascination. This man she had known for years, and yet did not know at all, was her husband. He had the right to lie there beside her. She now carried his name, just as she wore the ring that he had slipped on her finger during the ceremony in the chapel.

Remembering the ring, she lifted her left hand and studied the unusual piece of jewelry carefully. Although wide, it had a delicate look because of the filigree design. She had never seen anything so beautiful, nor so unusual. When had Cody gotten it? Had he known that he was to marry her tonight? Somehow she didn't think so, although he had hidden his reaction well.

With a soft sigh, she closed her eyes and allowed her body to relax. She could hear the sound of Cody's soft, even breathing and was surprised to find it reassuring as she drifted off to sleep.

The next time she opened her eyes they widened in surprise. Dawn light filtered into the room. Cody was watching her as he lay beside her, propped on his elbow, his head resting in his hand. She gazed up into those blue eyes of his, which had haunted her dreams the night before, and saw an expression there that she'd never seen before.

"Good morning," he murmured, slowly lifting his hand and with his finger nudging a wisp of hair away from her cheek. "Did you sleep well?"

She blinked. She had never heard that particular tone in his voice, either—it was warm and sensuous and caused her body to quiver.

Carina nodded, unable to speak.

He began to run his fingers through her hair as she began to relax.

"I'm afraid I can't say the same," he replied in a low voice, filled with self-mockery. "I kept waking up to find myself in bed with this beautiful woman. Despite all the rumors to the contrary, that just isn't my life-style. I found it downright disturbing." He grinned at her and she saw the teasing twinkle in his eyes.

"I found it a little strange, myself," she admitted.

He moved his hand to the side of her face and trailed his fingers along the curve of her cheek, traced the line of her jaw and down the length of her throat, eventually pausing at the demure neckline of her cotton nightgown. Mesmerized, Carina neither stiffened nor attempted to pull away. As though encouraged by her lack of objection, he slowly leaned down and pressed his mouth gently against hers.

Carina could feel something inside of her letting go, as though a part of her were melting. Quivery sensations rippled through her body in gentle waves causing her to shiver. Cody shifted slightly and slid both of his arms around her.

Carina felt engulfed in a swirling sea of feelings, all of them new, different and exciting. She shyly placed her arms around Cody's shoulders, and slid her fingers into the silkiness of his hair.

He made a deep sound of pleasure, delighting and encouraging her, so that she allowed her hands to explore him more fully, from the broad expanse of his back to the hair-roughened texture of his chest. When her fingers accidentally brushed against his nipple he shuddered.

Cody untied the ribbon at the neckline of her gown, loosening the garment so that it slid off her shoulder, exposing her breasts.

Carina knew she was blushing. How could she not? No one had ever looked at her so intimately before.

Cody lowered his mouth to her throat, leaving a trail of kisses to her breasts.

She forgot to breathe when he first touched his tongue to the tip of her breast. She had never known how sensitive that part of her body was until now. Exhaling on a shaky breath, she ran her fingertips across his chest with a sense of wonder.

"Ah, Carina," he whispered, inching her nightgown down, until she was fully exposed to his gaze. "You are so lovely. How could I have ever thought of you as a child? You are a woman—a perfectly formed...enticing...heart-stopping...woman." He interspersed his words with soft kisses on her breasts, her stomach, her belly button, her abdomen....

She stiffened at this newest intimacy, but he murmured soothing sounds while his fingers continued to work their magic over her body. She sighed and shifted restlessly, allowing her knee to fall to the side.

Cody leaned over her, finding her mouth again, no longer hiding his passion. She returned his kiss with innocent abandon.

His hands, never still, began to massage and circle at the top of her thighs where the melting sensations seemed to grow stronger. She wanted something more, something only he could give her, but she didn't know what that could be.

She whimpered and, as though he understood, Cody slipped his finger into the waiting softness. She gave a little jolt of delight and surprise at his audacious move. She lifted her hips to him in an unconscious rhythm, wanting to continue feeling the indescribable sensations he aroused inside her. His movements quickened, his tongue repeating the steady rhythm he had begun lower. She shifted, wanting to be closer to him. He increased the pace of movement until she felt a searing shock sweep through her, causing her body to stiffen like the bow of a hunter. She let out a soft, keening cry of surprise and release.

Carina couldn't believe what had happened just now. Cody held her tightly, stroking her hair, murmuring something beneath his breath. She listened, trying to hear his words, until finally she understood that he was apologizing to her.

She pulled away and looked into his eyes. "Why are you sorry?" she asked, when she could find her voice.

"For taking advantage of you. I didn't mean to let this go so far. It's just that—" his eyes burned, still hot with passion "—I've never been in such a situation before. I thought I had more control, but I—"

"Are you saying that what we did just now was wrong?"

"Well, no. Not wrong. Just, uh, inappropriate under the circumstances."

"We are married, Cody. You have done nothing that a husband would not do with his wife, have you?"

"Of course not. I mean, well, look, Carina. I'm older, more experienced, and I should know better. I don't want to take advantage of this situation. Neither one of us wanted to get married, but the fact is, we are."

She studied him for a long time in silence. "You don't want me," she finally said in a low voice, as though thinking out loud.

His laugh was not one of amusement. "Honey, if I didn't want you so damn bad, I wouldn't be hurtin' right now. But that's not the point. We barely know each other. You know nothing about the world. I know too much. You're an innocent, and I don't want to destroy that innocence." He rolled away from her and sat up, reaching for his jeans. "But I came damn close and I'm not very proud of myself."

"What are we supposed to do?" she asked to his back, as he stood without turning around.

"I wish to hell I knew," he finally muttered, stalking into the bathroom and slamming the door.

Six

———

"Carina," Cody drawled, dropping his arm companionably around her shoulders, "I'd like you to meet Letitia Callaway, better known in the clan as Aunt Letty."

They stood in the middle of a glass-enclosed room with a view of a patio that eerily resembled the one at Alfonso's hacienda. Carina smiled at the older woman who had been watering plants when they walked into the room. The woman registered surprise when she first saw them standing there. The surprise rapidly became shock, when Cody continued.

"Letty, my love, this is Carina Ramirez Callaway...my wife."

"Your—! Cody! What are you talking about?" Letty strode toward them, frowning.

Cody grinned his familiar lighthearted smile. A quick glance told Carina that the smile never reached his eyes. "I know, Letty, I know. You would have been there, if you'd known it was going to be a wedding. Well, I have to tell you...it took us all by surprise, didn't it, *chula?*" He gave Carina's shoulders a slight squeeze.

"I am very pleased to meet you, Miss Callaway," Carina said politely. "Cody has told me so much about you."

"Hah! I just bet he has," Letty replied with a snort. "And none of it any good, I'm sure." She looked at Cody for a long moment, then shook her head. "Married! Of all things! You were the very last person I would have guessed would be gettin' married any time soon."

Cody laughed. He sounded a little more relaxed now, which eased Carina's tension a little.

"This is a beautiful room, Miss Callaway. I—"

"My name's Letty...you might as well get used to saying it." She studied Carina for a long moment. "Carina, is it?" Shaking her head with resignation at Cody, she said, "She's just a child."

"She's older than she looks, Aunt Letty," he replied. "I thought she was about sixteen or so, myself, but she's twenty."

"I'm not talking age and you know it." Letty took Carina's hand. "I bet you're still attending classes, aren't you? In some private girls' school?"

"Not exactly, although I went to a private high school. I've recently finished my second year at the university in Mexico City."

Letty eyed her doubtfully. "Your family let you live there alone?"

Carina could feel herself flushing. "Well, not exactly. Alfonso rented an apartment for my mother and me. One of his men stayed there with us and drove me to and from school."

Letty glanced back at Cody. "About as close to convent-bred as you can find in this day and age. You ought to be ashamed of yourself."

"Dammit, Letty, I haven't done anything wrong. I tried to explain to Alfonso but he—" He stopped, running his hand through his hair. "Ah, hell. Why do I even bother trying to explain? It's too late, anyway."

"I would like to remind you, you uncouth renegade, that your language is not acceptable in the presence of ladies." With that Letty tugged on Carina's hand and said, "Come, my dear, let me show you around the Big House. I'm certain you would like to see your new home." Letty turned her back on Cody and drew Carina with her.

Cody stood there watching the two women leave the room. How in the hell did that woman manage to reduce him to a stammering schoolboy with visions of his mouth being washed out with soap? He could stand up to a kidnapper with a gun, he could face the dangers of working among drug smugglers, but Letty could ruffle his composure every time.

No matter. He was home now, with all that word signified. Letty was a part and parcel of the surroundings. Carina would have to get used to her, so she might as well start now. In the meantime, he would go get their bags.

They had stayed at Alfonso's hacienda that morning long enough for Carina to point out what she wanted packed and shipped to her in Texas. Since neither one of them wanted to see Alfonso, they had stayed upstairs to oversee some of the packing before venturing into the other part of the hacienda.

When they finally came down with their luggage Alfonso was nowhere around, which suited Cody just fine! To think that he had always considered Alfonso his friend. Some friend, betraying his own sister like that—forcing her to marry....

Cody paused, the trunk of his small car halfway raised, suddenly struck by something. He was angry at Alfonso, not because Alfonso had forced *him* to marry as much as because Alfonso had forced Carina. He lifted the bags from the car and closed the trunk, his mind caught up in his own reactions. Absently picking up the bags, he nudged the front door open and walked inside, heading for the wide stairway to the second floor.

Carina was the one who had been treated unfairly...like a child, without regard for her thoughts or feelings. None of the women he knew, from his aunt to his sisters-in-law, would tolerate such treatment. Of course, she had been upset. Who wouldn't have been?

As if that weren't enough, she had assured him that she wanted his life to continue as it had before, even though her dreams of an education and career had been dashed.

He was halfway down the hallway when he heard Letty's voice and was reminded of the suite of rooms in his wing of the sprawling house. Oh, no! He had meant to explain— He needed to—

The word he muttered beneath his breath was short, profane, and worthy of a vigorous mouthwashing.

He paused in the doorway of his room and leaned against the doorjamb, listening as Letty explained.

"Now this is the master suite in Cody's wing of the house. The dressing area is in here . . ." Cody watched the women disappear into another room, but he could still hear the tour guide's strident tones. "The bathroom is really quite something. Cole had all the plumbing updated and the fixtures remodeled a few years ago. If you ask me it was a big waste of money, gettin' all these fancy things, but then, again, I have to admit I've enjoyed my tub that swirls hot water around so briskly. After I've spent a few hours in the garden, that Jacuzzi-thing feels pretty good."

Cody shook his head, grinning. Letty had never admitted to anyone else, as far as he knew, that she approved of anything about the remodeling. What an old fraud she was!

When the women walked back into the room, Carina was the first to spot him. She stopped, looking at him uncertainly.

"Oh!" Letty exclaimed. "There you are. It took you long enough. Carina tells me most of her things are being shipped, which makes some sense, I'd say. I told her Rosie could help her unpack, but she insists she can do it."

She glanced at the two of them, who were continuing to stare at each other in silence.

"Well. I'm certain you two could eat something. I've never heard Cody turn down food. I'll just go down and tell Angie you're here."

Without taking his eyes off Carina, Cody murmured, "You do that, Aunt Letty. We'll be down in a few minutes."

He straightened to let her pass him, then hooked his heel around the door, letting it close behind him.

Carina started toward him. "I, uh, didn't know what to say to your aunt when she showed me this room. I mean, it's obvious it's yours and I don't want to take your room away. After all—"

"Carina?"

"Yes?"

"Stop worrying about things, all right?" He slipped his hand to the nape of her neck, feeling the weight of her long, silky hair against the back of his hand. Slowly, but steadily he pulled her toward him until he had both arms around her. He brushed his lips against hers once...twice...and then settled them more firmly, as he tasted and teased her delectable mouth.

She had tensed beneath his hand when he first touched her, but had not resisted when he pulled her closer. With his kiss, she seemed to relax and melt against him, as though she trusted him.

Trusted him! Cody jerked away from her as though he had been burned. With his hands on her upper arms he watched as her thick black lashes slowly left their resting place on her flushed cheeks and fluttered open, revealing those damnably compelling black eyes. His gaze wandered down to her mouth, still moist from their kiss.

Cody groaned.

"What's wrong?" she asked.

He just shook his head.

"I know I'm not experienced, but if you would show me how you want me to kiss you, I could—"

"Honey, you don't need any lessons, believe me. You do quite well on your own. Either that, or you're a hell of a fast learner."

He turned away, his shoulders stiff, and walked over to the window.

"Are we going to share this room?" she asked, after several minutes of silence.

"Not if I can help it," he muttered under his breath.

"Did you say something?" she asked.

He turned back to her, hoping he had himself under better control. "We'll work out something, *chula*. I don't know what we're going to do just yet." Afraid to touch her for fear he couldn't control his reactions, he said, "Let's get something to eat. I never can think on an empty stomach." He waved his hand to indicate she should precede him, so that he had the excruciating pleasure of walking behind her down the hallway and stairs, the view of her delectable derriere, swaying in front of him, a constant reminder of what he wanted but knew better than to pursue.

Good old Alfonso—his buddy, his pal—had a lot to pay for.

Letty joined them for lunch, which eased the tension for Cody. As usual, Letty had jumped in with both feet to help them manage their lives.

"I hope this means you intend to hang around the ranch more, Cody. Now that you've got a wife, you can't continue to gallivant around the countryside all the time, whoopin' it up with all your wild friends."

"What a lovely picture you paint of me, Aunt Letty. I'm touched."

"Surely you don't intend to drag Carina along with you. She would be—"

"No, Letty. I don't. I'm still thinking about what we can do now that we're married. You have to admit the circumstances are unusual. I mean, most people who get married have had time to adjust to the idea, make plans... that sort of thing. This whole business was kind of sprung on us."

Letty turned to Carina. "What were you planning to do before all of this happened?"

"I really didn't have any plans. When Alfonso refused to allow me to continue my education I stayed at home, helping around there."

"Why in tarnation wouldn't he let you finish your schooling?"

"He said I didn't need any more education. That I would marry and have a family and be busy with them."

"That's the biggest bunch of hogwash I've ever heard. Why, an education is just as important—maybe even more important—if you're going to be training young minds, than if you were out working somewhere."

Cody added, "What Carina wants to do is work in the field of speech therapy."

"Oh?"

"She was telling me that she had hoped to convince Alfonso to send her to school in the Chicago area."

Letty turned from gazing at Carina sympathetically and narrowed her eyes toward Cody. "So why don't *you* send her?"

"What?" He replaced his coffee cup in his saucer before he spilled its contents.

"You heard me. From what you were telling us, this gal risked her neck...and lost her reputation... trying to save your ornery hide. And what does she get for it? Stuck here with a footloose husband and a bossy old woman."

"I wouldn't consider you exactly old, Letty," Cody drawled, grinning.

"Don't get smart-mouth with me, now. Do you intend to settle down and stay here at the ranch full-time?" She leaned on the table and faced Cody without blinking.

"I don't know if I can, Letty. You see, I—"

"Oh, I see a lot of things, young man. Mostly I see that you don't have the sense God gave a goose. Carina is without a doubt the best thing that could have happened to you, and you don't even know it. She went from one domineering, opinionated man to another."

"Hey, wait a minute. I'm nothing like Alfonso. I'm not telling her what to do. I married her, damn it, I didn't purchase her. She's got a mind and a will of her own. She can do anything she pleases. You make it sound like I intend to chain her up in my room or something."

Letty's harshly lined face seemed to crinkle, then crack. Cody stared at her in shock as the lines rearranged themselves into a big grin, as she said, "Prove it!"

In all the years he had known Letty, Cody couldn't remember seeing her smile so broadly before. Oh, there had been a few times when the corners of her mouth might quirk up for a split second, but Cole had once suggested it was no more than a gas pain. Cody stared at his aunt as if she had just turned from a frog into a prince . . . or in this particular case, a princess.

"Prove it?" he echoed, thoroughly confounded.

"That's right. Let's see you put your money where your mouth is."

"Meaning?"

"If you're so all-fired liberated that you won't stop your wife from doing what she truly wants to do, then why don't *you* send her up to Chicago to school?"

Cody stared at his aunt, convinced she had finally cracked after all these years. Her eyes sparkled and she sat there, still smiling at him, as if the joke were on him, if he could just see it.

Letty had always liked to get the best of him. He took pride in the fact that she rarely managed to do so, and he wasn't about to admit that she might have gotten the upper hand this time.

"Actually, I've been thinking along those very same lines, myself." He lied, with commendable self-possession given the existing circumstances. "However, I haven't had an opportunity to discuss the matter with Carina." He glanced at his watch. "We've barely been married twenty-four hours. I assumed we would take a few days to, uh, to—"

"Honeymoon?" Letty asked.

"Well, no. Not exactly. I mean, there's no reason to rush into a— Dammit, Letty. It's none of your business, and I don't even know why I'm discussing it with you. Whatever we decide will be between us, do you understand? I—"

"Cody?"

Carina's soft voice punctured his ire, releasing the build up of steam into a sizzling hiss that escaped from his lips. He turned to his wife. "Yes?"

"Were you really thinking about sending me to school?"

Her eyes sparkled with hope and with excitement. He looked into their depths and was lost. His gaze flickered to her lips and down the graceful line of her neck. He swallowed. "Sure... if that's what you want."

"Oh, Cody! I can't believe it. Last night I thought my dreams were over, that I would never be happy—"

There was no doubting her sincerity. It played hell with his ego. He had been escaping the clutches of possessive women his whole life. He had lost count of the number of women who had done everything in their power to get him to make a permanent commitment to them. Each time he had run, feeling nothing but relief that he had managed to escape. Now his wife could hardly wait to get away from him.

He didn't like the feeling that gave him. It left a bad taste in his mouth. He took a bite of Angie's cherry pie and *slowly* chewed, in an effort to buy himself some time.

Of course Letty had to jump back in. The two women were already considering phoning the university, to see if she could still register for the spring semester. They talked about getting records transferred, about appropriate clothes for that far north, about a place to live.

"Cody, why don't you two buy a place up there? There's no reason to rent, when you could own a place."

"While you're arranging my life so swiftly, Letty, you might want to take into consideration that I would have nothing to do in Chicago."

Letty waved her hand in dismissal. "Of course, you wouldn't. I wouldn't expect you to stay up there. Just help Carina get situated. She's going to be too busy to look after you, anyway. This way she can concentrate on her studies and you can practice curtailing some of your more outrageous activities—if you have a mind to, that is."

"Well, thank you for the invitation to plan a little of my own life."

"Oh, quit puffing up like some ol' horny toad, Cody. You're not the sulkin' kind. Besides, this is all your idea, anyway. Didn't you just say so?"

"Buying a place in Chicago didn't suddenly pop into my mind, no."

"Well, of course, that's up to you. But it's just such a waste to pay rent, when you can own a place. Then Carina could fix it up any way she pleased and not have to worry about some fussy landlord."

He looked from Letty to Carina. "Would I at least get to have visiting privileges?"

Carina stared at him uncertainly, then smiled. "You're teasing me, aren't you?"

Slowly he grinned at her. "Yeah, I think I am."

"You don't mind if I go to Chicago?"

He sighed, confused by all the conflicting emotions that had been running through him during this conversation. Less than twenty-four hours ago he had been incensed that a bride was being thrust upon him. Now he was feeling abandoned because she was blithely planning to stay out of his life.

Wasn't this what he wanted?

He could continue his work unhindered. He could attend Enrique Rodriguez's trial, keeping Carina's involvement to a minimum because of the distance. He could, in effect, retain his bachelor status, at least for another year or two.

"No, *chula*," he said after a long silence. "I don't mind if you go to Chicago. I think it's a great plan. I want you to be happy. I want you to be a person in your own right, not just my wife."

Carina came around the table and hugged him, her eyes moist with happy tears. "Oh, thank you, Cody. I am so happy...thanks to you."

He hugged her back, his eye caught by the pleased look on Letty's face. When she saw him watching her, she winked and gave him a thumbs-up signal.

Her approval made him feel a little better.

But not much.

Seven

"Oh, Cody, look at the view! I had no idea Lake Michigan was so large. It could be the Gulf of Mexico."

Cody sauntered over to stand beside Carina and look out the plate-glass window of the condominium. "You'd notice a difference if you were in it. This is freshwater...the Gulf is saltwater."

"Oh, this is so beautiful. What do you think, Cody?"

He hadn't taken his gaze off his wife. "About what?"

"Do you like the apartment?"

He glanced around. "It's all right, I guess. A little small."

"Small! Cody, it has over two thousand square feet. That's huge."

"I suppose. Guess I'm used to the Big House."

She walked across the massive living room and disappeared through the kitchen doorway. "This kitchen is wonderful," she announced. "I can't believe it. A place to myself. I can spend all the time I want in here."

He followed her to the doorway and looked inside, watching as she opened cabinet doors, the refrigerator and oven doors, and checked the microwave and dishwasher. When she caught him staring at her she laughed. "I feel like I'm in a fairy tale."

"Oh, yeah? Which one, *Beauty and the Beast*?"

She shook her head, her eyes dancing. "Of course not. *Cinderella*!"

He blinked. "Are you saying you see me as some kind of prince?"

She danced over to him and hugged him. "Oh, yes. You make a wonderful prince, Cody. Tall and very handsome and—"

His mouth covered hers, effectively muffling her next words. Once again she melted against him, a habit that increasingly frustrated him. Damn! He wanted this woman like none he had ever known. In just a few weeks, she had insinuated herself into his life so completely that he couldn't remember what he had done without her.

He was aware of every breath she took, every movement she made. He listened for her delighted laugh, finding ways to provoke it. He found excuses to touch her—brushing a wisp of hair away from her face, running his hand over her shoulder, hugging her—and as often as possible, kissing her.

He felt like an addict, craving a fix.

Meanwhile, she treated him like an indulgent uncle.

She pulled away from him with another hug, and said, "Are we going to buy this one?"

They had looked at dozens of places and time was running out. After a flurry of paperwork and phone calls, Carina was enrolled in school. Finding a place for her to stay was a must.

"Do you think you could be happy here?"

"Oh, yes!"

"I'll admit I like the security in this building. Would you be afraid to stay here alone?"

She shook her head. "But I won't be alone all the time, will I?" She looked wistful.

"Of course not. It's just that I can't walk away from what I'm doing right at this time. I've already extended my leave twice. As soon as I get you settled, I've got to head back to Texas."

She spun away from him and headed down the hallway toward the bedrooms. He had already looked at them. There was a large master bedroom with private bath, another bedroom that would serve as a guest room, also with private bath, and the third could easily become a study.

He followed her into the master bedroom. She stood in the middle of the room turning in a small circle. "Oh, Cody, we need furniture, and dishes, and linens and— I can't believe how much."

"Don't worry about it. We'll go tell the realtor we've decided on this one. It shouldn't take long to sign the papers. We'll spend the next couple of days shopping. I thought women enjoyed that."

"But we're spending so much money," she pointed out.

"*Chula,* I've got three trust funds that I've never touched. I've never had to. In addition, I get a third of everything generated by Callaway Enterprises. Don't worry about breaking me. It won't happen.''

She came to him and took his hand. ''But it's all your money. I've contributed nothing.''

''Alfonso sent the papers to transfer the money he had been investing that your father left for you. You're not exactly a pauper, darlin'.''

''Could I have control of it?''

''Certainly.''

Her eyes widened. ''Aren't you going to tell me how I don't know anything about managing money?''

He grinned. ''Don't worry. You'll learn—one way or the other.''

''Oh, Cody, I am so happy and it's because of you. Then I feel so guilty. I've been given so much, while you've gotten nothing.''

He picked up her left hand and kissed the wedding band she wore. ''What do you mean, I've gotten nothing? I have a wife. That's good enough for me.''

She stared at him doubtfully. ''Are you sure?''

Once again, he pulled her into his arms. ''Don't ever doubt it, darlin'. I wouldn't have it any other way.''

Their hotel suite had two bedrooms and Cody had not allowed himself to think about entering her bedroom there. He had promised her time... and space... and he was determined to give it to her, even if it killed him. He had never heard of anyone dying from too many cold showers, but there was always a first time.

Now they would have a place of their own. He liked the feeling that gave him. Oh, he loved the ranch. He had a special feeling for the land, a feeling that neither Cole nor Cameron seemed to share. They were content to establish homes elsewhere and occasionally visit the Circle C.

He had always known he would spend his life living on the ranch, but he was just now realizing that he liked owning a place that was just his and Carina's. Since she planned to continue her courses through the summer, she would get her degree in eighteen months.

Although he would need to continue what he was doing on the border until the present operation was concluded, he would still be able to fly to Chicago to see her on a regular basis. Thank God for the company jet; he wouldn't have to plan his visits around an airline schedule.

Letty had been right to insist that Carina be given a chance to make her own decisions. Cody was enthralled with Carina's blossoming personality. Free of restrictions for the first time in her life, she seemed to float—her obvious joy encompassing everything and everyone around her.

Cody could get lost in the moment, if he were to allow himself. He could forget about all the promises he had made to her and to himself. He could become a permanent part of her life.

Did he dare?

A week later Cody let himself into their new apartment. He had been out at Midway Airport talking to the pilot and arranging his flight back to Texas. Now he had the unpleasant duty of telling Carina that he was leaving tonight, although he knew she had been expecting him to leave any day.

Last night had been their first night in their new home. When it was time for bed, Cody had taken the coward's way out and slept in the guest bedroom.

What the hell was wrong with him, anyway? He was acting like some adolescent kid with his first crush, stammering and stuttering, feeling awkward and ridiculous.

Carina hadn't said anything about the sleeping arrangements to make him think she wanted him to stay with her. Somehow he had gotten himself all tied up in the situation, needlessly complicating what was really a simple relationship.

They were adults, weren't they? Surely they could sit down and sanely discuss the matter. Of course they could...soon. In the meantime, he would continue his role of casual companion, at least for this last night they would have together for awhile.

Cody paused in the doorway, his gaze drawn to the dining alcove. His heart sank at the sight that greeted him. The small round table had been draped with a lace cloth, silver candlesticks held flame red candles already lit, their bright color matching the red roses he had given Carina two days ago—on her first day of classes. Now they were arranged in a low bowl between the candles, seductively scenting the air.

Their new china, crystal and silverware sparkled in the candlelight, and red linen napkins were intricately folded on the plates.

A tantalizing scent of savory ingredients drifted from the kitchen.

Cody groaned. How was he going to be able to maintain a semblance of casual companionship in an atmosphere like this?

"Cody? Is that you?"

"It had better be," he replied, pocketing his key and moving toward the kitchen.

Carina came out of the kitchen and met him. She wore a filmy, full-skirted dress with long, flowing sleeves and a high, ruffled neckline.

"You look sensational."

Her face lit up. She glanced down at the pink dress. "Oh, do you like it? I wanted something special, but I'm not used to buying clothes on my own." She touched the sleeve. "I was hoping it was all right."

He took her hand, brought it to his mouth, and placed a kiss across the knuckles. "It is more than just all right. You have exquisite taste. If you don't believe me, just look around you. You have an innate sense of style."

Draping her arm over his shoulder, he pulled her closer, eager to kiss her. A loud buzzing sound erupted in the kitchen.

"Oh! The roast is ready. Are you hungry?" she asked, stepping away from him. In a whirl of flowing material she fled to the kitchen.

"Oh, yeah. I'm very hungry," he offered, more to himself than to her. He felt as if he were starving for another taste, another touch. He would be leaving her in a few hours, with no idea of when he would return. How could he possibly walk away without—

Carina came out of the kitchen carrying a laden tray. Cody reached her in two long strides, taking the heavy weight and carrying it to the table, where she placed the separate serving dishes in their designated areas.

She took the tray from him and headed for the kitchen. "I bought some wine today," she said over her shoulder. "Would you like to open it?"

He followed her into the kitchen. "My, you *are* being daring. Wine, yet!"

He listened for her chuckle, and smiled to himself when he heard it. "If you must know, I explained what we were having for dinner and the nice man suggested some wines. He let me sample them, so I would know the one I liked best."

"What nice man?" he asked suspiciously.

She handed him the wine. "The one at the liquor store."

"Humph." For a moment he had envisioned his naive little wife blithely accosting some stranger on the street. He should have known better.

Cody discovered that he actually had an appetite for food as soon as he began to eat her meal. "I had no idea you could cook," he said, pausing to sip the wine. He had to admit that she had made an excellent choice.

"Are you being insulting?" she asked, raising her brows.

"Not intentionally. Why?"

"I thought every young girl was taught how to cook. How else can she supervise what goes on in her kitchen?"

"Most of the women I know admit they get lost in a kitchen."

"Really?" Never had her smile appeared sweeter. "But then, it wasn't their cooking skills that attracted you to them, was it?"

He almost choked on his wine. He felt just like he suddenly had been clawed by a baby kitten he had been stroking gently. "I was paying you a compliment," he pointed out with dignity.

"By comparing me to your other women? Not likely."

"Hey, what are we talking about here? I don't have any other women."

She eyed him for a moment over her wineglass. When she finally put the glass down, she asked, "You don't?"

He kept his gaze steady. "No. You are my wife. There is no one else in my life."

"But I'm not your *real* wife. I mean, it isn't as though you chose me or wanted to marry me, or—" Her voice trailed off.

Cody pushed his chair back with careful movements and stood. Then he walked behind her chair and slid it away from the table. When she looked up at him he grinned, saying, "And if you're going to add that I don't want you, then you're wrong, *chula*. Very, very wrong." He picked her up—his arms around her waist and beneath her knees—and started down the hallway toward the bedrooms.

"Cody? What do you think— We're in the middle of dinner, Cody. Why—"

His mouth effectively silenced her. He could taste the wine on her lips, smell the scent of her new perfume, feel her tremble, hear the catch in her breath, and when he lifted his head, he could see the smile of encouragement on her face.

Knowing that she wanted him pushed him over the edge.

Even in his urgency, he carefully removed her dress and matching slip, her hose and shoes, until only her bra and panties remained. He undressed, breaking all of his previous records for speed, then knelt beside her.

"You are so beautiful," he whispered, spreading her hair over the pillow... trailing his fingers along the edge of her bra . . . sliding his hand behind her to unfasten that particular garment.

"I feel beautiful when you look at me that way," she admitted. She sounded a little breathless. And shy.

She shivered when he lifted the bra away. With his finger he lightly touched the pink crest now revealed, watching it draw into a tight nub. Cody leaned over and flicked his tongue across the rosy peak. She shifted restlessly.

He reached beneath her and pulled the bed cover and sheet down, then over her. "Are you cold?" he whispered. She shook her head, but her skin continued to ripple with goose pimples. "Let me warm you," he murmured.

He fought the clawing need deep in his belly, determined not to rush her, not to take advantage of her as he had on their wedding night.

He ran his hand across her body and down her side—soothing and yet arousing, reassuring and encouraging her to respond to him.

She was so sweet. He could no longer resist kissing her. This time he placed his kisses all over her body as he explored her, memorized her, possessed her with his lips.

"Oh, Cody, oh, please . . . I want you to— Oh, yes, please . . ."

When he moved over her and allowed her to feel how strongly she affected him, she lifted her hips in silent supplication. How could he resist such honesty when he wanted her equally as much?

He bent her legs and knelt between them, then slowly leaned forward until he was stretched out over her, resting his weight on his forearms. She pulled him down so that she could kiss him, her mouth searching, her tongue imitating the motions he had taught her.

She was small…small and so tight he was afraid for her, but she wouldn't let him draw away. Instead, she locked her heels together around his thighs, forcing him to complete what he had started.

He felt her flinch when he broke through the thin barrier and he hated himself for hurting her, but, oh! she felt good. He felt her warmth surround and enfold him. Never before had Cody experienced anything like this.

There was no more time to savor the spiraling sensations. He had waited too long, spent too many restless nights, endured too many cold showers to deny himself for another moment.

Each movement made him groan with pleasure and when she seemed to go up in flames all around him he lost the small amount of control he had maintained. He joined her in the conflagration.

Not wanting to crush her, he rolled until she lay on top of him, still joined. He pressed her against him, enjoying the slight weight of her, as she cuddled so intimately against him.

He couldn't seem to keep his hands still. As though they had a mind of their own they continued to stroke, to fondle, to caress, until he could feel himself growing hard inside her once again.

She lifted her head and stared at him, her eyes wide in astonishment. He grinned and slowly lifted his hips, causing her to gasp. She was still sprawled across him. Lazily, he positioned her knees on either side of his hips, then eased her away from him until he could find her breast with his mouth.

She tightened her knees, hugging him with her thighs, and he began to move in a smooth, rhythmic motion. His hands rested on her hips, guiding and mutely instructing her.

He wasn't at all certain that he ever would get enough of her, not if he tried for the next hundred years.

She was so perfect, this small, innocent person. His wife.

Carina took over the rhythm, increasing her movements until he was wild, straining, fighting for and yet not ready to accept the culminating release that was rapidly overtaking them.

When the release struck, Cody felt as if he were drained from his toes upward, leaving nothing but a shell. He couldn't believe what had just happened. He had never been able to reach two such dizzying climaxes in such a short time. What had this woman-child done to him?

He lay there, gasping for air, wondering if his legs would ever be strong enough to carry him out of there.

"Carina?" He managed to get out after two tries.

"Mmm?"

"*Chula,* there's something I meant to tell you," he paused between every two words in an effort to find air enough to talk.

She raised her head and looked at him. "We're not married?"

Her question caught him off guard and he choked, laughing. When he was finally able to speak again, he said, "As far as I know we're definitely, legally married."

"That's nice," she murmured, allowing her head to rest on his chest once more. "I'm very, very glad."

He could feel the slight movement of her hand caressing him, and his heart seemed to swell in his chest with new and overwhelming emotion.

"I don't want to leave you," he admitted.

"Then stay," she replied softly, not looking at him.

"I can't. I meant to tell you earlier, but seeing you and—and well, everything, made me forget. I'm leaving tonight. I should have been at the airport an hour ago."

She jerked her head up and stared at him. "Tonight?"

"Yeah. Now, as a matter of fact."

She glanced down at the two of them so closely entwined, and grinned. "Like this?"

He shook his head, a feeling of despair slipping over him. Never had he felt so pulled in opposite directions. He had given his word that he would return tonight. He needed to be in Mexico no later than tomorrow night. He had spent years infiltrating this particular group and there was no one to take his place. He had to be there.

But not now! he wanted to cry out. Not when he had moved his wife fifteen hundred miles from where he would be. He reminded himself that she would be much safer up here. He also reminded himself that she needed this time on her own, needed to know that he would not be oppressive and dictatorial as her brother had been.

"You never finished your dinner," she finally said.

"I know. You were just too distracting," he admitted ruefully.

She sighed and shifted, allowing him to sit up. "When will you be back?"

He headed toward the shower, not trusting himself to look at her and still have the strength to leave. "As soon as I can possibly get away. You can count on that."

Eight

Cody stared out the window of the plane at the clouds drifting past the wing tip, feeling as though he had spent most of the past eighteen months in the air between Texas and Chicago. He had thrown himself into his work in an almost desperate effort to bring about a successful conclusion to the sting operation the DEA had set up with his help.

He ran his hand over his face. The past two weeks had been hell. He couldn't remember the last time he had been in a bed for a full night's rest. He had gotten into the habit of napping wherever he could, in whatever was available at the time—a chair, a couch, a bench. When he finally got a couple of days' break, he had grabbed it, taking time for only a quick shower and some clean clothes.

He closed his eyes, his thoughts on Carina. He hadn't seen her in almost six months, the longest they had been separated since the wedding. Six long, grueling months.

Even their telephone conversations had proven to be frustrating. One of her first questions when he called would be, When was he coming to see her? Invariably his answer would be painful for him. He didn't know. After that, she would have little more to say, merely answering his questions in monosyllabic words.

She didn't understand what he was doing and why it was so important. He couldn't tell her the whole truth. In the past few months Alfonso had become a part of the scene, which had devastated him. Alfonso, part of the drug cartel? How could Cody tell his wife that he was diligently working to put her brother behind bars?

Never had Cody so misjudged a man as he had Alfonso.

Alfonso had sent several messages to Carina through Cody, but she never made any comment when he passed them on to her. Cody had kept his distance from Alfonso, using his supposed attitude regarding the forced marriage as an excuse for his continued aloofness. What a hell of a situation to be caught up in! Worrying about Alfonso, and Carina's reactions, had been the cause of a great deal of his sleeplessness these past several months.

He felt so isolated. Somewhere in the time since he and Carina had married, Cody had discovered that he no longer wanted his self-imposed isolation. How ironic that he now had no choice.

He closed his eyes, entertaining himself with memories of their times together during her first year in Chicago. He smiled to himself, allowing his mind to drift and to dream....

* * *

If he were to single out the most anticipated moment of each visit, it would be that instant when she first saw him. He couldn't begin to describe the rapidly changing expressions that raced across her face, but joy seemed paramount.

Another welcomed event was waking up with her in his arms each morning. He never grew tired of that aspect of their relationship. On the contrary, he could hardly wait until the time they would be together every day and every night for the rest of their lives.

Each trip he had made north had brought them a little closer. Resisting his need to keep her in bed with him for his entire stay, Cody virtuously had planned outings for them. Sometimes he would take her shopping, delighting in buying her things she would not buy for herself. They attended movies, plays, museums, and explored the many aspects of the city.

However, he much preferred the times when they were alone.

He found her shyness endearing. As responsive as she was during their lovemaking, she never initiated anything, always waiting for him to show her what he wanted from her. He smiled at some of those more intimate memories and stirred restlessly in his seat. Although she appeared prim and dressed very properly—even at home—she came alive in his arms.

He was looking forward to their time together these next few days. He felt as if he were escaping from the reality of his life and indulging in a fantasy where there was no evil to combat and conquer.

Carina had done well in school. She would be graduating in a few weeks, thank God, and would be returning to Texas. Unfortunately, everything on the border was heating up. The timing for her return was all wrong. One of his reasons for breaking away now was to talk to her about her plans.

His boss knew he would be finished with this type of work once this sting operation was concluded. Cody hoped that he would never have to tell Carina what he had been doing in Mexico nor the part he had played in Alfonso's arrest.

He had decided not to tell her he was coming on this trip since he had canceled two of his previously planned visits. She probably wouldn't have believed him, anyway.

He had decided to go directly to the campus and wait for her to finish with her classes. They would go home together and make up for the months they had been apart.

He could almost feel the silkiness of her long hair as he ran his fingers through its thick length. He fell asleep with a smile on his lips.

Carina stopped to speak to her instructor before leaving the classroom. There were only three more weeks before finals. She was excited and filled with anxiety at the same time. For several minutes, the instructor discussed with her some of the points she had raised, then Carina left the room and started down the hallway.

She would never regret having moved to Chicago and continuing her education. Her internship at a local speech clinic had already convinced her she had chosen the right field, but at what price?

The move might have cost her her marriage. What marriage? she reminded herself. For the first year she had been here she had kept herself so busy she didn't have time to miss Cody when he wasn't there. Back then, he had flown up to see her every few weeks, seemingly as eager to be with her as she had been to have him there.

They never talked about their feelings for each other. She was too shy to tell him how much she had grown to love him, especially when he showed no indication of wanting to hear such a declaration. He was so self-assured, so self-sufficient. She knew that Cody Callaway needed no one, not even a wife.

He showed her a great deal of attention whenever he visited. She blushed at some of her memories. She had discovered some things about men as her circle of friends increased. She better understood their needs and drives, and knew that Cody could want her without necessarily loving her.

Most of the time she could accept the truth of their situation. Other times, she felt lonely and bereft.

She had been so upset the last time he had canceled his proposed trip to see her that she could scarcely talk. As soon as she had hung up from that conversation, she had burst into tears and cried for hours.

Why did life have to be so complicated? Surely to be in love with your husband wasn't such an unusual circumstance. She shook her head in an effort to break her chain of thought.

"Carina? Hey, Carina, wait up."

She glanced over her shoulder and saw Chad, one of her classmates who worked with her at the clinic.

"Hi, Chad. What's up?"

"I'm walking these days. My car finally gave up the ghost last week and went to that old parking lot in the sky." He piously held his hands beneath his chin in a prayer-like position and looked heavenward. "My buddies and I had a ceremony for the old geezer. That car was older than I was, you know. It was more like a friend. We'd been through a lot together. To commemorate the loss, Charlie made a wreath of empty oil cans and Dave said an eulogy at the junkyard.''

Carina laughed as Chad held the door open for her. She ducked under his arm and stepped outside. The brisk breeze, so familiar to the area, whipped her ankle-length skirt around her legs.

She fought with her skirt and the loose hair blowing around her face at the same time.

''Need some help?'' he asked, laughing at her efforts.

She looked up at him and saw the teasing glint in his eye. ''I can just imagine what sort of help you would give me!''

He obligingly wiggled his brows in a mock-villain way and growled, ''You are safe in my presence, me beauty, never doubt that.'' Chad dropped his arm around her shoulder, effectively holding her hair in place. ''Where you headed?'' he asked, matching his steps with hers.

''Home. I don't have to go to the clinic until Monday. How about you?''

''I'm supposed to be at the clinic within the next half hour. I was hoping you were going that way so I wouldn't have to take the bus, but—''

''No problem, Chad. The clinic isn't that far out of the way. So what did you think about the prognosis on the Moreno child?''

They talked about their assigned cases as they wended their way across campus, comfortable with their casual companionship.

Cody watched them coming toward him. They were so absorbed in their conversation they were oblivious to their surroundings.

He hadn't recognized her at first, because he hadn't expected to see her with anyone—especially not a man. An icy dread seemed to fill his chest. The cozy way she was tucked under the guy's shoulder irritated him, but he wasn't going to jump to any hasty conclusions.

Once she saw him, he would know.

So he waited beside her car and watched the couple approach him.

Carina raised her head after finding her keys in her purse and saw Cody casually leaning against her little sports car, his legs negligently crossed at the ankles, his arms folded across his chest.

"Cody?"

Her face registered shock. Nothing more.

"Cody! What are you doing here? Why didn't you call and let me know you were coming?"

Cody watched her shrug the man's arm from her shoulder and hurry toward him. He was glad he wore his sunglasses; they masked the pain he knew must show on his face. Slowly, he straightened to his full height.

"Hello, Carina."

She stopped a few inches away, not touching him. "How did you get here?" she asked in a breathless voice.

"Took a cab. Thought I'd surprise you." He glanced past her. "Guess I did, huh?"

She spun around. "Oh! Cody, this is Chad Evans, a classmate of mine. We work together at the clinic. Remember I told you I've been putting in twenty hours a week there this semester?"

"I remember." He held out his hand. "Cody Callaway."

Chad took his hand and grinned. "Oh, I knew who you were. I've heard about you from Carina."

"Oh?" He glanced down at her. She watched him without expression. There was no sign of welcome in her face, no indication that she was glad to see him. The icy dread in his chest grew larger. "I'm afraid you have the advantage, then. Carina's never mentioned you."

Carina spoke up. "I've offered Chad a ride to the clinic. He's temporarily without transportation."

"Hey, no problem," Chad said, backing up a couple of steps. "You didn't know your husband was here. I understand how it is. You've both got a lot of catching up to do. Look. I'll take a bus and—"

"Don't be silly," she said. "If you don't mind the tiny back seat, you won't have to wait for a bus in this blustery weather." She looked at Cody with a level gaze as if she were expecting him to make a comment. Instead, he stepped back and waited for her to unlock her car.

Carina and Chad kept up a spirited dialogue on the way to the clinic, making Cody feel old and totally out of touch. The two students obviously shared friends and associations that meant nothing to him. He rubbed his raspy jaw, wishing he had shaved.

Why hadn't he gone directly to the apartment and gotten some sleep, rather than rushing to the campus like some lovesick swain wanting a glimpse of his own true love after months of being away from her? He felt a little foolish given the circumstances.

He had wanted her to experience freedom. He had wanted her to feel as though she had had a choice. Had she already made her choice? Did it include him?

They pulled up in front of a small whitewashed building. Cody crawled out of the car so that Chad could get out of the small back seat. Once he stood on the curb, Chad held out his hand. "I enjoyed meeting you, Cody. I don't have to tell you what a special person Carina is. You're very fortunate."

"I think so," Cody replied quietly. He waited for Chad to turn away before he got back into the car. "I think this car shrinks every time it goes through the car wash," he grumbled, fastening the seat belt and straightening his legs.

She smiled. "It's a fun car for me, though. It's just my size. I've enjoyed having it, even if I did try to talk you out of buying it for me. You were right."

"I'm glad you're enjoying it."

"Where would you like to go?"

He sighed. "I haven't given the matter any thought. All I could think about was getting here."

"You look tired," she said, studying him.

"Yeah."

"Then we'll go home and I'll make you a good dinner. Can you stay long?"

This was worse than anything he had imagined. He had braced himself for her irritation, ire, anger. Instead, she was treating him like an acquaintance, with aloof politeness.

"A couple of days," he mumbled. He leaned his head back against the headrest and watched as she efficiently guided the car into the flow of traffic and headed downtown.

He loved watching her hands. They were so small, so graceful. He loved to feel the silkiness of them, the—

"Carina?"

She gave him a quick glance, as though she heard a new note in his voice. "Yes?"

He stared at her hands and realized that he didn't want to know. But he had to ask. "Why aren't you wearing your wedding ring?"

"Oh, I was in a hurry this morning. I took it off to put some cream on my hands and forgot to put it back on."

"Does that happen very often?" He kept his tone as casual as he could.

"Does *what* happen often?"

"Forgetting to wear your ring."

"I haven't really thought about it."

She didn't say anything more for several blocks, and Cody decided to leave the subject alone. He was too tense and tired for a rational discussion and she was in a mood he had never seen before.

They parked in the underground parking lot beneath the building and rode the elevator to their floor in silence. He pulled out his key and opened the door. Once inside, Carina headed toward the kitchen. "I'll start dinner," she said over her shoulder.

"Carina?"

She stopped. With seeming reluctance she turned back to face him, but said nothing.

"What's wrong?"

She raised her brows. "I don't know what you mean."

"You're different."

"From what?"

"From the way you usually are when I come see you."

She crossed her arms. "Perhaps I am. Nobody stays the same, Cody. We change. We grow. We become different people. You, of all people, should know that."

"What's that supposed to mean?"

"A wife was a novelty to you, at first. Playing at marriage was a game, setting up house together, hurried visits back and forth. And then you stopped coming." She turned and went into the kitchen.

He followed her to the door and leaned against the doorjamb, his hands in his pockets. "I'm here now."

She began pulling items from the shelves, the refrigerator, the cabinet. "I know," she murmured, pulling out a knife and beginning to chop the vegetables in front of her.

"You don't seem to care."

She jerked her head up and looked at him. "Oh, I care, Cody. That has been the problem for me. I care. I miss you. I want to see you. You promise to come, then beg off. I feel as though I'm hanging in limbo, not knowing what to do, how to plan. Yes, I have my freedom, but only to a degree. I am part of a marriage that isn't a marriage. I have a husband whom I rarely see. What do you expect from me?"

He shrugged. "I suppose I wanted you to be happy I managed to get here."

Slowly, she put the knife down and came toward him. Sliding her arms around his neck she went up on tiptoe and whispered, "I am very happy you are here, Cody," just before her lips pressed against his.

Cody grabbed her and held her tightly against him, desperate for her. He teased her mouth open and plunged his tongue inside, showing her how much he had missed her, how much he wanted her, how empty he had felt.

The kiss went on and on, until Cody thought he was going to explode. He lifted her in his arms and carried her to the bedroom, peeling their clothes away, feverishly touching and tasting, exploring and caressing, his breath harsh, his longing almost devouring him.

She responded almost as feverishly. Cody lost all coherent thought, lost in the passionate present, surrounding himself with this woman who had become more important to him than life itself.

Their passionate coming together rapidly escalated, crescendoing into cries of release, and they clung weakly to each other as if they were survivors of a tempestuous storm that had almost destroyed them.

For long minutes they lay there. Cody felt drugged, unable to think beyond the moment. Eventually their surroundings impinged on his consciousness, and Cody realized he hadn't bothered to pull back the covers. They lay across the spread with total disregard for the delicate fabric.

He nuzzled her ear. "I've missed you, *chula.*"

"I've missed you, too."

"I'm sorry everything's so mixed-up right now."

She pulled away so she could see his face. "Mixed-up?"

"With my job and everything. My project should have been completed months ago, but it keeps dragging on and on."

"This job is very important to you, isn't it?"

"The commitment I made to stick with it is, yeah."

She sighed, then rolled away from him.

"Where are you going?" he asked, leaning on one of his elbows.

She pushed her hair behind her shoulders and walked away from the bed. "To get a shower and finish the meal I started."

Cody watched her bare backside until she closed the door to the bathroom. What was going on? She had been with him every step of the way in their lovemaking. How could she walk away with such seeming indifference now?

For the first time in his life he felt used, then discarded. He hated the feeling...and he hated the dread that had taken up permanent residence in his chest.

He went into the other bathroom and showered. When he returned to their bedroom, he found an old pair of his jeans and a shirt he'd left from one of his previous visits.

He found Carina in the kitchen. She was wearing a satin lounging robe of sapphire blue. Her hair was haphazardly piled on top of her head, with curling wisps falling around her ears and the nape of her neck. She looked adorable to him. She also looked aloof.

By unspoken agreement they kept their conversation casual, mostly limited to putting dinner together, his flight, her classes. Neither seemed to want to discuss anything personal.

Dinner, as usual, was a delight. Cody savored every bite, feeling the strain and weariness slip away from him while they ate. Carina made coffee and they sat in front of the fireplace while they enjoyed their after-dinner drink.

Once again Carina's attitude and actions denoted a shift in their relationship. In the past they had sat on the couch together, where she generally ended up in his lap.

Tonight she sat in one of the matching wing chairs.

He lounged on the couch and watched her gaze into the small fire he had started earlier. Her profile fascinated him. He wished he were an artist and could capture the purity of her face—the way her nose tilted upward so slightly at the end, the clean line of her jaw and patrician neck. The soft glow of the firelight brushed her cheeks. Her mouth... He almost groaned at the wave of feeling that washed over him when—

"Cody?" she asked in a husky voice, still gazing at the fire.

"Mmm?"

"Did Aunt Letty ever get in touch with you?"

"About what?"

"My message."

"No. I haven't talked with her in a while. What was the message?"

Her smile was sad. She still didn't look at him. "It is no longer important."

"Tell me, anyway."

When she turned her head, he caught his breath in shock. The pain reflected in her eyes caught him totally unprepared.

"A few months ago I tried every way I knew how to contact you without alarming your family. I needed you so much, but I couldn't—" Her voice broke and she looked away for a few moments before continuing, "I couldn't find you anywhere."

Cody sat up, leaning forward, his elbows resting on his knees. "What happened, *chula?* Why were you looking for me?"

She bit her bottom lip, in an obvious effort to gain control. After swallowing a couple of times and taking a few deep breaths, she said, "I had a miscarriage four months ago."

Cody shot off the couch and was leaning over her before he was conscious of moving. "Oh, Carina, no! I didn't know. How—?" He reached for her and saw her stiffen. Stricken by her instinctive reaction, he carefully moved away from her and sat down on the couch once again. "Will you tell me what happened?"

She looked down at her hands folded in her lap. "I didn't even know what was wrong at the time. I'd been spending long hours at the library doing research work. I hadn't been feeling well for several weeks, but I thought I had the flu. I missed you so much and you had already called once to say you weren't going to be able to come to Chicago, after all."

She paused, but for the life of him Cody couldn't think of a single word to say. She had been alone and had needed him, and he hadn't been there for her.

"What happened?" he asked gruffly.

Her eyes were steady when she said, "I was at the library and started having terrible abdominal pains . . . like cramps, only so much worse. The librarian called an ambulance and I was rushed to the hospital, but there was nothing anyone could do. They kept me in the hospital for two days. That's when I tried to reach you. I didn't want to alarm Aunt Letty, so I just asked her to have you call me if she heard from you. I gave her the number, but didn't tell her it was a hospital. I never heard from you."

Once again she looked down at her hands. "When I got home I was so upset. I felt guilty because I hadn't known I was pregnant. I blamed myself for not questioning the symptoms sooner, even though the doctor said there was nothing I could have done to prevent what had happened.''

"Oh, God, Carina. I'm so sorry." He wanted so much to take her in his arms, to hold her. He hated to think of what she must have gone through all alone. The pain must have been devastating. The shock of the news was slowly giving way to his own sense of loss for a child he had never known existed.

"I thought we were being so careful," he murmured, almost to himself. "I thought—" He stopped, shaking his head.

"I've done a great deal of thinking about our situation since then," Carina continued, her voice firmer. "For the first time I realized what it meant to be independent and on my own, truly on my own." She gave him a small smile that almost broke his heart. "It has taken me a long time to grow up...much longer than most women my age."

When she looked at him again, he could see the inner strength that she had drawn from these past few months. "I've been blaming Alfonso for my situation, but I can no longer do that. Alfonso was acting from the highest motives. He was protecting me from my own foolishness in thinking you needed to be rescued. You and I have both paid the price for my poor judgment, and for that I'm sorry." She looked back at the fire. "I'm sorry for many things, but not for the opportunity to get to know you better, to be your wife, to grow up."

Cody wanted to interrupt, to explain to her that— What could he explain? That she had been brave to act in the way she had? That she had touched him in a way that no other human being had managed to do?

"I've been offered a job here in Chicago, Cody," she continued, "with the clinic where I've been working this spring. At first, I told them no, but they insisted I consider their offer for a few days. So I have been. And what I realized is that I don't want to go back to Texas and live at the ranch if you're not going to be there. I am willing to commit to this marriage, but only if you are."

"Otherwise?"

"I will stay in Chicago and allow you to continue the life you so obviously want."

"Does this mean you want a divorce?" Cody was surprised to hear his voice sound so calm, when his heart was pounding so hard in his chest he felt his breath was being shaken out of him.

"That would be up to you."

"I don't want a divorce," he stated harshly.

"What do you want?" she asked softly, her gaze on him.

Cody came to his feet, unable to sit still. He began to pace. "I want us to be together. I want us to have a home...and a family." He pivoted on his heel and stared at her across the room. "I love you, Carina. I love you with all my heart."

She stared at him, obviously shocked, and he realized this was the first time he had ever said the words out loud...to anyone.

Slowly she came out of her chair and walked over to where he stood by the large plate-glass window. When she reached him, she took his hand and raised it, pressing her lips to his palm. "I love you, too, Cody. It seems as though I've loved you for most of my life."

She stared at his anguished expression. "But it doesn't really change things, does it? Not for you, anyway. Your work comes first."

"I was doing this work before I ever met you. I've told you that. All of this happened with you at a time when I was least prepared to have a relationship with anyone. I can't just walk away from my job...not at this point in my investigations."

She closed her eyes for a moment.

"Do what you must, Cody. I won't try to stop you, because I know it would do no good."

"What about you, *chula?* Will you come back to Texas?"

She had never released his hand. Now she placed another tender kiss in his palm, carefully folded his fingers over the kiss, and let go of his hand.

"No, Cody. I cannot sit and wait for your occasional visits, with nothing to occupy my time when you are not there. I'll stay in Chicago. Perhaps some day we will be able to arrange our lives to better suit our desires. In the meantime, I have an opportunity to do the work I have trained for."

"It won't be for much longer," he said eagerly, then dropped his head back and stared at the ceiling with a groan. "How often have I said that since we've known each other?" he muttered in frustration. Looking at her once again, he said, "We can work this out, *chula.* I know we can. We love each other."

She turned and looked out at the night. "Sometimes I wonder if love is enough."

Nine

One Year Later

Carina rushed through the side door of the clinic, already late for her next appointment. No doubt the waiting room was full. She had spent too much time at the hospital this morning, but she had needed that time to reassure the parents of six-year-old Jamie that he could be taught to speak again.

She pulled off her coat and started down the hallway.

"Carina! Thank God you're here."

She paused by the receptionist's desk. "I know. I'm going to be backed up for the rest of the day."

"It's not that. Your brother-in-law has called twice. He wants you to call him right away. He said he tried the hospital but you had already left, so he called back here."

Carina felt as though a giant hand had grabbed her, squeezing all the air from her lungs. She forced herself to battle the shock that had swept over her with Helen's words. "My brother-in-law?" she repeated in a careful tone.

Helen handed her a slip of paper. "Here's the number where you can reach him."

Numbly Carina took the pink slip and stared at it. Helen's excellent penmanship carefully spelled out the name Cole Callaway, the date and time of each one of his calls, and a number.

"Thanks," she mumbled, turning away.

"I hope nothing's wrong," Helen responded.

"So do I," Carina replied.

Her heart thudded in her chest, hammering at her ribs. Why would Cole be calling her?

She had not seen or spoken to Cody's family, with the exception of Aunt Letty, since her wedding. She had no idea what they thought of her continued stay in Chicago. She and Cody had never discussed their reactions.

Nevertheless, she knew she felt defensive. How could anyone understand that she and Cody had chosen to live apart, to live separate lives with minimal contact between them?

There were times late at night when she lay awake staring at the ceiling, wondering where he was, what he was doing and with whom. Carina had doubted the wisdom of her choice to remain in Chicago, but had to continue to remind herself that she would have been just as alone at the ranch with nothing to occupy her time.

She glanced at the slip of paper in her hand. She wasn't at all certain that she was ready to hear whatever Cole wanted to say to her. Since he had never made an effort to contact her before now, the matter must be urgent—to have prompted him to call the hospital and her office looking for her.

Had something happened to Cody? They had only spoken by phone a few times during the past few months.

Perhaps Cole was just relaying a message—a message that Cody had chosen not to give her directly.

She sat down at her desk and picked up the phone, her hand shaking. She had to start over twice before she got the right sequence of numbers. The phone rang once before it was answered. The deep voice sounded enough like Cody to increase her heartbeat even more.

"This is Carina Callaway," she managed to say, relieved to hear that her voice sounded a great deal more calm than she felt.

"Carina! Thank you for returning my call so promptly. I wasn't sure—" He paused, as though unwilling to finish that statement. His next words paralyzed her.

"I wanted to let you know that Cody's been hurt. I'm afraid I don't know much about the details. He was flown from McAllen late last night to a San Antonio hospital. He's in surgery now. I came to Cam's office to try to notify you. The rest of the family is at the hospital."

She kept trying to swallow the lump in her throat. "How bad is he?" she forced out.

His silence was worse than anything he could have said. Finally, in a voice rough with emotion, he replied, "Not too good. A bullet caught him in the chest, another in his hip. They weren't certain of his other injuries."

"You mean he's been shot?" Her voice rose and she immediately fought for control. "I thought he was in an automobile accident. What happened? Where was he? Who—"

"I'm afraid I don't know any more of the details...just that it happened in Mexico and that someone down there had enough authority to get him across the border so that he could be taken to a hospital here in Texas." He paused, and she realized that he was fighting for control, as well. "They, uh—" there was a long pause before Cole continued "—they almost lost him on the flight up here."

Carina jammed her fist against her mouth to stifle the cry that came to her lips. When she could trust herself to speak, she replied, "I'll be there as soon as I can get a flight."

"The jet's on its way to Midway Airport. It should be landing there within the hour."

"Thank you, Cole. Thank you for calling."

There was a moment of silence before he said, gruffly, "I thought you would want to know."

She squeezed her eyes in an effort to hold back the tears that threatened to fall. "Yes," she managed to say before they hung up. Carina couldn't let go of the phone, but continued to sit there hanging on to the only link, however tenuous, she had with Cody.

Forcing back the tears, she stood and carefully picked up her purse—as though she could hold the shock of Cole's news at bay by concentrating on practical details.

She paused at Helen's desk. Taking a deep breath, she forced herself to speak calmly. "Helen, I'm afraid I've got to leave." She forced herself to take another couple of breaths before she continued. "My husband—'' her voice squeaked and she stopped, gnawing on her bottom lip ''—has been hurt. I must go to him,'' she managed to get out.

''Oh, Carina, I'm so sorry! I'd hoped it wasn't bad news. Is there anything I can do?''

Carina closed her eyes, trying to think. After a moment, she said, ''You'll have to rearrange the appointments, see if there's anyone available to cover mine. I don't know when I'll be back.''

''Let us know how he's doing, all right? And don't worry about anything here.''

''Thanks, Helen.''

Numbly Carina went through the motions as she drove herself home. She thought about all the shopping she had done these past few weeks, all the plans she had made in her determination to reestablish her marriage.

Why had she taken so long to make up her mind that Cody was more important to her than anything else in her life? Why hadn't she made more of an effort to find him and tell him that she was coming back to Texas, had already given her notice of resignation at work . . . that she loved him and wanted to be with him, regardless of his other commitments?

She pulled into the underground parking lot at the apartment, got out and hurried to the elevator. Once she reached the apartment she paused, forcing herself to think about what she would take.

Carina pulled some clothes out of the closet and tossed them onto the bed, opened drawers and emptied them, searched for shoes and other accessories. Then she went into the bathroom and gathered her personal items and threw them into a cosmetic bag.

She retrieved her luggage from the hallway closet and began to pack, all the while praying, "Hang on, Cody. Please hang on. I'll be there as soon as I can. Oh, darling, don't leave me now that I've finally realized how much I need you."

Less than an hour after she had talked with Cole, Carina was on her way to Midway Airport. The sleek jet was being refueled when she arrived. She was used to bringing Cody to the airport to catch the plane. This would be her first time to fly alone. She grabbed her suitcase and hurried across the Tarmac.

The pilot met her at the top of the steps. "Here, Missus Callaway. Let me have your bag."

"Thanks, Sam." The muscles in her arm leaped and jerked after having the weight removed from that arm. She went over to one of the seats and thankfully sank into it, strapping herself in.

"Do you need anything before we take off? It'll be about another fifteen minutes or so."

She shook her head, closed her eyes and rested her head on the headrest.

Her mind kept racing around, filled with questions that couldn't be answered. What could have happened that would have caused Cody to be shot? He would never tell her exactly what he did, just referred to investigative work. Why hadn't it ever occurred to her that he might be involved in something dangerous, especially after the night she had heard those men plotting to kill him? He had later explained that the man who had kidnapped them had a vendetta going against the Callaways and now that he was behind bars with a long-term sentence, there was nothing more to fear.

She had believed him.

"Oh, Cody, please be all right."

She couldn't imagine what the world would be like without Cody somewhere in it. She loved him so much...loved him as a woman now, and not as the child she had once been.

She looked down at the gold wedding band that gleamed on her left hand. She touched it lightly with her other hand. She remembered how upset he had been to discover her not wearing it. She had been childish to take off the ring the day after her miscarriage, out of spite, anger and pain.

His strong reaction had made her ashamed of herself. Since that day she had never taken it off again. During the ensuing months of loneliness, of waiting for his phone calls, of wondering how much truth there had been in his declaration of love that last weekend they had spent together, the ring had represented hope to her. He had given it to her, insisted she wear it despite their continued separation, as though the symbol of their marriage had some magical quality for him. Sometime during the passing months she had begun to feel the same way.

She heard a noise and opened her eyes. The pilot stepped inside the plane and closed the hatch, then disappeared into the cockpit. Soon she felt the vibration and heard the sound of the plane as they prepared for takeoff. She waited, eventually feeling the thrust of the small plane's power engines as it rapidly built up speed, then lifted away from the ground, quickly gaining altitude.

This was the hardest part, when there was nothing to do but to sit and wait...and remember. She closed her eyes again and remembered the way Cody looked the first time she saw him, all golden and glowing with vitality and life.

"Please take care of him, God," she whispered. She touched the ring as a talisman and waited to reach her destination.

Cameron and Janine met her at the airport in San Antonio.

"How is he?" were her first words when she stepped off the plane.

"He's hanging in there," Cameron responded. "The surgery went well, according to the doctor, but there was considerable damage. If your brother hadn't acted so quickly, Cody would never have gotten out of there alive."

They were walking toward Cameron's car. Carina stopped walking and stared at him. "Alfonso? Are you saying that Alfonso was there when Cody was shot?"

With a slight tug, Cameron urged her forward. "That's right. He's at the hospital now."

Carina couldn't take all of this in. She had neither seen nor spoken to Alfonso since the night she and Cody married. She had resisted every overture he had attempted. She had kept in touch with her mother through letters, but had made no attempt to see her because of Alfonso.

And now he was at the hospital!

Once in the car, Janine said, "I almost didn't recognize you when you stepped off the plane. You made a lovely bride, but wow! Look at you now."

Carina smiled, knowing that Janine was trying to distract her. "It's probably just the hair. Once I started to work full-time I decided to find a simpler hairstyle.'' She ran her fingers through her hair that fell in soft curls around her face, ears and neck.

"That's part of it, I suppose. But you look so—oh, I don't know what it is...sophisticated, maybe, uh—"

"Sexy?" Cameron suggested with a sly grin at his wife.

Janine laughed. "That, too. Has Cody seen your new hairdo?"

"No."

Cameron and Janine exchanged glances but said no more.

At the time she had her hair cut off, she had wanted a completely different look. Obviously she had achieved her goal. Her clothes were considerably different, as well. She felt as though she had finally moved into the twentieth century, wearing bright colors and current fashions.

She knew that part of the change was to give herself more self-confidence. She liked her new look. In her present concern for Cody, she had forgotten that he had not seen her new appearance. From Cameron and Janine's reaction, perhaps she should have warned him.

It was too late now, but it probably wouldn't matter. No doubt they had exaggerated their reaction in an effort to get her mind off Cody.

"Have you seen Cody since he was brought in?" she asked, leaning toward the two people in the front seat.

They pulled into the hospital parking lot and parked. Cameron replied, "No. He was still in recovery when we left to go to the airport." He opened her door and helped her out of the car. She walked between Cameron and Janine, comforted by their presence, needing others who loved Cody around her. They rode together in silence up to the proper floor and when they stepped off the elevator she saw Cole and Alfonso standing at the end of the hall, talking. Both men turned and watched her as she approached.

Alfonso had aged considerably during the past couple of years. His hair was almost completely silver now, and there were deep furrows across his forehead and down his cheeks. When he saw Carina his face brightened with surprised recognition and love that had her choking with sudden emotion.

This was her brother...the man who had raised her, nurtured her, protected her. He was here now, at a time when she desperately needed emotional support.

With a small cry she ran into his open arms. He held her tightly, his face buried in her hair, and they clung to each other for timeless moments before Carina lifted her head and looked up at him. Tears streamed down his face and she stared at him with wonder. She had never before seen Alfonso cry.

"Cody?" was the only word she could force past the lump in her throat.

"They have him in intensive care, still heavily sedated," Cole said from somewhere behind her. "They're allowing one person at a time with him for a few minutes once an hour. I was in a few minutes ago."

"How was he?"

Cole shook his head. "I can't tell. They have him hooked up to all kinds of machines. His chest and thigh are heavily bandaged, one side of his face is swollen and discolored. He looks like he's been through a rough time."

Carina looked at her brother. "Cameron said you were the one who brought Cody here?"

Alfonso nodded. "Yes. I was just explaining what happened to Cole."

Cole said, "Look, why don't the two of you stay here and catch up on everything while we go get something to eat. We won't be gone long."

Alfonso answered. "All right."

"Can we bring you something?"

"Nothing, thanks."

Carina watched the Callaways walk away, then felt a slight tug on her arm. She glanced around.

"There's a small waiting room over there that's empty," Alfonso said and led her into the well furnished room.

"Can you tell me what happened?" she asked, sinking into one of the chairs.

Alfonso sat down beside her and took her hand. "Yes. It is time that you should know."

She watched him as he rubbed his hand over his face.

"For years," he began, "Cody and I have been working at cross purposes." He paused for a moment. "It's been a case of the left hand not knowing what the right hand was doing."

"I don't understand."

"Are you aware of what Cody was doing in Mexico?"

"Investigative work, he said."

"Do you know who he was working for?"

"No."

"The United States Drug Enforcement Administration."

She stared at Alfonso in bewilderment. "Cody is an agent?"

"Yes . . . working undercover."

"Oh!"

"What you need to understand is that I've been doing the same kind of work for my own government, deeply undercover."

Carina stared at him as if she had never seen him before. How could she have been so unaware of yet another similarity between her husband and her brother?

"So we began to watch each other, suspect each other, until we finally learned the truth."

"When did you learn the truth?"

"A few weeks ago."

"You thought he was a drug dealer?"

"Of course not. I thought he was Cody Callaway of the Texas Callaways who enjoyed flirting with danger. Only as all our plans began to fall into place and come to a head did our bosses see fit to inform us that as brothers-in-law we were also working for a common purpose."

She glanced down at her hands. "Cody never told me."

"He couldn't."

She looked up at him. "But you can?"

"Now I can, because it is over. We successfully completed what we set out to do. After considerable time, difficulty and tremendous effort, we were able to gather several members of the cartel together where they could be arrested."

"Is that when Cody was shot?"

Alfonso sighed. "Unfortunately, yes."

How could he have been doing something so dangerous for so many years without her knowledge? During the years Cody had come to visit with Alfonso, he had joked and teased with her, as though he never took anything seriously.

"Those men I overheard?" she finally responded.

"Ah, yes. We were able to trace them eventually. They had been hired by Enrique Rodriguez to follow Cody and report his whereabouts. My men knew them and thought I had hired them, but I knew nothing about their being on the premises until several weeks later."

"Were they involved in the drug war?"

"Not really. They were hired guns willing to do most anything for a few extra dollars."

"Does Cody know they were identified?"

"Oh, yes. He never lets anything rest until it's resolved. He came to me with the information when he had proof. That was one of the many times I tried to contact you in hopes of getting you to accept my apology for what I had done to both of you."

"Cody accepted your apology?"

"He didn't seem to care. He was more interested in the fact that we had located and captured the men." He looked away from her for a long moment before returning his gaze to her. "I need to tell you that Cody was shot because of me."

"You had him—"

"No, no. Please don't misunderstand. I was the one who told the cartel members they were under arrest. Agents from both countries immediately stormed the room, but one of the drug men pulled his gun. Cody leaped between us, knocking me to the floor and catching the bullets meant for me."

Carina stared at him, tears running unheeded down her face.

"I immediately yelled for help and worked to stop the bleeding. We had helicopters standing by to transport prisoners out of there. We managed to have Cody airlifted out of there as well and flown across the border, then transported here."

"Why? Why would he have done such a thing?" she asked, almost to herself.

Alfonso sighed. "I asked him the same thing, before he lost consciousness."

"Did he answer you?"

"Yes. He looked at me and said, 'Because Carina loves you.'"

Ten

***

"**M**rs. Callaway?"

Most of the family was there in the waiting room when the nurse appeared in the doorway, but everyone knew which Mrs. Callaway was being addressed. Carina came to her feet, her eyes on the woman's face. "Yes?"

"You may see your husband now."

Carina was trembling so hard she could scarcely stand. "Thank you." She glanced around the room at Cole and Allison, Cameron and Janine, Aunt Letty and Alfonso. Each of them gave her a soft word or nod of encouragement, giving her strength to follow the nurse out of the room.

They walked down one of the hallways and through a pair of swinging doors marked *ICU No Admittance,* then into one of the rooms. Carina moved slowly over to the bed and looked down at Cody. She fought for control. This was even worse than she had imagined. No one could have prepared her for the shock of seeing him lying there, his skin gray. If the various machines surrounding him had not been making their steady beeping sounds, she would have thought he was dead. Only his hair gave off a certain brightness against the starkness of the pillowcase.

He was attached to a series of wires and tubes. She was almost afraid to touch him for fear of dislodging something. Gingerly she picked up his hand and lifted it to her lips.

"I love you, Cody," she whispered.

He didn't stir, but then she hadn't expected a response. She had just needed to say the words to him.

He had saved her brother's life. Despite everything that had happened, he had known how much she loved Alfonso. How could he have sacrificed his own safety to save her brother? Didn't he know how much she loved him, too?

"I sincerely hope this means that your work in Mexico is finished," she whispered. "I'm going to be very selfish, my darling, and insist that you spend more time with me. I need you so much."

The nurse came back in a few minutes and Carina left. But only because she had to. She had every intention of returning as often as possible.

She loved this man, and she would do whatever necessary to preserve their relationship.

Cody felt as though he had been trampled by a herd of elephants. Angry elephants, at that. One of them seemed to be resting its foot on his chest, pinning him to the ground. He moaned and attempted to change positions, causing pain to shoot through his hip and down his leg.

In the midst of his agony, someone took his hand and brushed it against something soft and warm. He fought to open his eyes, then blinked in an effort to clear them.

Where was he, anyway?

Carina's beautifully shaped black eyes stared back at him. He smiled, or at least he made the attempt. His face felt stiff and swollen. He watched her place a kiss on his knuckles and realized he was now witnessing what he had felt a few moments ago.

Carina. She was so often in his thoughts that he found nothing unusual about seeing her beside him now. He had been dreaming about her only a few moments ago.

"Hi," he tried to say, but his throat was too dry. He licked his lips and tried again. "Where are we?"

"A hospital in San Antonio."

He frowned at that news. San Antonio? What was he doing there? The last thing he remembered was—what? where? He closed his eyes in an effort to concentrate.

"The doctor said you're doing amazingly well. He's quite pleased with your progress."

Good for the doctor. What sort of progress had he been making? "What are you doing here?" he finally asked, opening his eyes once more.

"Being with you."

"Aren't you supposed to be working?"

"I took some time off."

"Oh."

He allowed his gaze to wander around the room, which was large and rather luxurious. He couldn't remember ever having been in a hospital before as a patient. Lying flat on his back was a new perspective. He wasn't at all impressed.

He closed his eyes, wishing the pain would go away. There was something important he needed to do . . . or say. . . .

"Carina?"

"Yes, darling?"

He must have said her name out loud. He smiled to himself and returned to that place where there was no pain. . . .

The next time he opened his eyes the room was dark except for a night-light. Carina was still there, watching him, a slight smile on her face. She looked . . . he searched for a word, wondering why his brain felt so sluggish. She looked . . . happy . . . yeah, that was it. Happy and content, as though her fondest wish had been granted.

"So what am I doing here?" he finally asked.

"How much do you remember?"

He thought about that for a while. "Not much. Was I in a wreck?"

"Not exactly."

"Then what?"

"I believe the official phrase is that you were injured in the line of duty."

"Line of duty—" He paused, thinking, and images began to appear. After several minutes of silence he sighed, "Oh, yeah. Line of duty." He looked around the room again, avoiding her eyes. "Was anyone else hurt?"

"No."

He closed his eyes. "That's good," he murmured, drifting away once more....

Light filled the room when he woke up again. Carina sat in the chair beside his bed. "Don't you ever go home?" he asked gruffly.

She had been reading a magazine until he spoke. At his words she looked up and smiled. "Once in a while, why?"

"I just wondered."

He shifted, trying to find a more comfortable position. "How long are they going to keep me in here?"

"Until you're well enough to go home."

"When will that be?"

"They haven't said." Carina picked up a glass of water. She held the bent straw to his lips. He managed to sip, enjoying the cool, refreshing feeling of the liquid as it eased his thirst.

He allowed his eyes to drift closed, when something different finally registered on his consciousness. He blinked his eyes open once more. "Your hair! What did you do to your hair?"

She tilted her head slightly before saying, "I had it cut off."

"I see that, dammit! Why?"

She eyed him, her expression sober. "Don't you like it?"

"Carina, I've always loved your long hair. I could never leave it alone. I can't believe you cut it off without even mentioning anything to me."

He sounded like a sulking child and he knew it. Damn, he felt so helpless. He hated lying there in bed, every movement taking an enormous amount of his limited energy.

"It will grow back, you know," she said after a moment.

He shut his eyes. "It doesn't matter. You've got your own life to live. I don't have any right to comment." That was what he thought. It wasn't how he felt.

After several minutes of silence, he searched for a new topic. "How's work?"

"Always there," she replied.

"Isn't that the truth? No matter how much you do, there's always something more that needs to be done."

"Is that what's kept you in the business?"

He raised one of his brows. "What business?"

"The undercover business."

"How did you know about that?"

"Alfonso told me."

He looked at her, trying to figure out her mood from her expression, but she was giving nothing away. "You spoke to Alfonso?"

"That's right."

"When?"

"After he brought you here. He stayed until you were out of intensive care, then he returned home."

"Did you ever forgive him for forcing you to marry me?"

"Yes."

He found himself smiling. "I'm sure he was relieved."

"I got the impression that you forgave him a long time ago."

He started to shrug, but the slight movement made him wince. He touched his bandaged chest and made a face. "I just didn't like the way he went about things, that's all."

"Why didn't you tell me the two of you were working together?"

"Because I couldn't. Besides, for the longest time I didn't know he was on our side. I thought he was one of them. I had to deal with the probability of arresting my own brother-in-law. My boss didn't have to be quite *that* secretive!"

"Speaking of your boss, I spoke to him when he came to check on you. He told me that you had put in your resignation effective as soon as you made these arrests."

"So?"

"So, it looks like you're now unemployed."

He thought about that for a moment, then smiled. The idea sounded good to him. Very good. "Looks that way, doesn't it? Guess I'll be able to spend some time with you now." He eyed her a little uncertainly. "That is, if you're willing to have me come." He glanced down at her hand and was surprised at the relief he felt when he saw her ring glinting on her hand.

He closed his eyes, not wanting to react to her, not wanting to feel what he always felt in her presence . . . a longing so intense that he ached with it for hours.

"You won't have far to travel."

His eyes opened. "What do you mean?"

"I've resigned my position. I talked with the office a couple of days ago. They've already found a replacement who can start right away. Looks like I'm unemployed, too."

Damn. He wished his chest would stop hurting. He struggled to push up on his elbows but couldn't handle the strain on his chest muscles. "Hey, there was no reason to quit your job because of what happened to me. I don't need you to—''

''I didn't quit my job because of what happened to you. I tendered my resignation at least four weeks ago. I had decided to surprise you with the news on our anniversary.''

''Anniversary?''

She grinned. ''Um-hm. We have an anniversary coming up in a few weeks. By the time you've done your physical therapy on your hip and allowed your chest to heal, I'm hoping you'll be well enough to leave the hospital and help me celebrate.''

He could feel an easing of an age-old pain in his chest. This one had not been caused by a bullet wound. No, he had carried this one ever since the day he had seen her coming across the campus with a guy named Chad.

''Is that what you want?'' he asked gruffly.

''More than anything I can think of,'' she replied, smiling, while tears trickled down her cheeks.

Several weeks later, Cody stood at the entrance of the hospital. He had finally been given a clean bill of health. His chest gave him a twinge or two now and then, and he still walked with a slight limp, but the doctor assured him that if he took it easy he would have no problems with the chest wound. The limp would disappear with continued exercise.

He had been in daily phone contact with Carina for the past two weeks. She had returned to Chicago to pack and have their belongings shipped to the ranch. She placed their condo on the market and tied up all the loose ends before making her move south permanent. Then she drove back, arriving home yesterday so that she could pick him up this morning when he was released.

He paused for a moment, filling his lungs with air, glad to be out of the hospital environment. He could have left before now, but his boss and doctors had insisted he rest and regain his strength. He knew he had been pushing himself for a long time now. He had been exhausted and run-down before all of this came to a conclusion.

He hated to admit that the doctors had been right. He hadn't felt this good in a long time, a very long time. Part of his mood was because he was going to see Carina. He hated going a day without seeing her. Two weeks had seemed like an eternity. Never again would he allow himself to go through the hell of not being with her for a year!

A car pulled up and he recognized it as Carina's car. He grinned and started down the steps, watching as the car door opened and Carina stepped out. Cody caught his breath and stared.

She wore a flaming red dress that lovingly displayed her trim figure and a pair of heels so high that she swayed when she walked. Three men across the street stopped to stare at her and one motorist came to a screeching halt before he hit the car in front of him, whose driver was straining to get another glimpse of her retreating form.

This was not the same woman who had been practically living at the hospital while he was there, wearing jeans and no makeup. Now she wore dark shades that covered the upper part of her face, somehow calling attention to her delectable mouth. Her lips looked soft and very kissable.

Slowly he made his way toward her, wondering if she was aware of the danger she presented to traffic in the area. From her expression, she appeared to be unaware of anyone but him.

She lowered her glasses and peered over their dark rims. Her large black eyes gazed up at him before she went up on her toes and kissed him oh-so-gently on the lips. She smiled at him and said, "If you would like, I can drive."

The men across the street shot him varying looks of admiration, irritation and envy. He could certainly understand their reaction. "That's quite a dress you're wearing, honey. It could set off a riot with very little provocation."

She laughed. "I bought it especially for today, sort of as a celebration. Do you really like it?"

"If we weren't in public, I'd show you exactly how much I like it," he replied in a husky voice. He rested his hand in the small of her back while they walked to the car.

After she helped him into the passenger seat, she walked around to the driver's side. Just as Carina opened her door, Cody heard a wolf whistle from some punk on a motorcycle. Then he became aware of Carina sitting down beside him in her short, snug skirt.

"It's a damn good thing I've got a strong heart, darlin'. Otherwise, I'd be going into cardiac arrest," he drawled, looking at the expanse of leg showing.

"Are you talking about my dress?" she asked, starting the car.

"Yeah, partly. There isn't much to it, is there? I mean . . . isn't it a little short?"

"C'mon, Cody. This is the style."

"Hmm. I wonder what your mother would think."

She adjusted her glasses without offering an opinion, then pulled out of the parking space. He kept watching her legs while she shifted gears, then his gaze wandered up to her face. "Thanks for arranging to get me out of there. Another day and I would have been clawing the walls."

"I told the doctor you would have round-the-clock supervision and attention, if he'd let me bring you home."

He grinned. "And what did he say?"

She glanced at him out of the corner of her eye. "You really want to know?"

Faint color filled her cheeks, which he found rather intriguing. "Yeah."

"Lucky fellow," she said, attempting nonchalance.

He threw back his head and laughed, then held his chest.

"Are you in pain?"

"Well, there's pain and then there's *pain*. Are we going to the ranch?"

"Uh, well, no. Cole suggested we go down to South Padre Island to the family condo for a few days. Since that's almost three hundred miles from here, I thought we would have a leisurely dinner, stay at one of the hotels tonight, then travel tomorrow. We don't have to be anywhere at any particular time, which is nice."

"Sounds like a good plan."

She gave him a quick smile, almost a nervous smile, he decided. He wondered what she was up to.

Hours later they sat sipping their coffee in the dimly lit restaurant. Once again Cody decided that Carina appeared to be a little nervous. Was it because they would be going back to the hotel soon?

If he didn't know better, he could almost imagine that his sweet little wife had intentions regarding him . . . seduction intentions. If so, he was going to sit back and enjoy watching her technique.

They finished their coffee while Cody admired the way the candlelight caressed the contours of her face. She picked up her purse and played with the catch for a moment. Finally she looked at him from beneath a thick fringe of dark lashes. "Are you ready to go?"

"Anytime you are," he replied, flashing her a smile that seemed to fluster her.

Cody placed money on the tray next to the bill and stood. He helped her out of her chair and motioned for her to walk in front of him. Once outside the restaurant he opened the passenger door and waited patiently while she got in, then quietly closed the door. When he crawled in beside her from the other side he said, "That is one eye-catching outfit you're wearing, *chula*. The only problem I have with it is the number of eyes it catches. Some of those men back there almost fell off their chairs when you walked by. I mean, I like short skirts, and I like snug-fittin' short skirts, but I'm not at all sure I like other men watching *my wife* in a short, snug-fittin' skirt."

"Are you saying that you don't want me to wear this dress?" The expression in her eyes gave him pause. He thought for a minute.

"No, ma'am, I'm not. What I *am* doin' is statin' my preference about some things. What you choose to do about what you wear is strictly your business."

Neither one of them said anything more. When they reached the hotel, he handed the car keys over to the parking attendant and escorted Carina inside. He was enjoying the exercise he had gotten today, but recognized that he didn't have his full strength back, which was frustrating. He was tired and didn't like it. Not at all, given the circumstances. He was with his wife and he had definite ideas on how he wanted to spend the evening, every one of them calling for energy and stamina. He absently rubbed his chest and sighed.

As soon as they reached their suite, Carina excused herself and went into the bathroom. Cody wandered over to the window and looked down at the river that wound its way through the downtown area of San Antonio.

After a few minutes he went into the bedroom. He heard water running and decided she must be taking a bath, which could take a while. He sat down on the side of the bed and took off his boots. Then he stripped off the rest of his clothes and stretched out, pulling the covers to his waist. After all his complaining at the hospital, he had to admit that there were times when a bed was downright useful. This was definitely one of those times.

After flipping on the television with the remote control he clicked through various channels. He didn't really care about watching television, but he knew he was a far cry from being ready to sleep. He didn't see that he was left with very many options from which to choose at the moment.

Although the water had shut off in the bathroom, he could hear soft, swishing movements and pictured Carina in the large tub, relaxing. He was tempted to offer to join her. After all, it wouldn't be the first time they had bathed together. Then he remembered his recent wounds and decided to wait a few more weeks to indulge in that particular exercise.

While he stared at the television screen he remembered the times they had spent together, which didn't help his state of mind nor other parts of his anatomy in the slightest.

He heard the bathroom door open some time later, but didn't immediately look around. Chastising himself for being a coward, he glanced away from the television only to discover she had not come out of the bathroom.

A wisp of scent teased him, and he recognized the cologne he had bought her on one of his trips to Chicago. He remembered the day they had chosen the seductive scent, as well as the evening when he had given her a physical demonstration of the various points on the body where cologne could be applied with tantalizing results.

He almost groaned out loud.

He clicked past three more stations and had paused to watch a commercial when she finally walked out.

Cody gave her a casual glance to let her know that—Every thought in his head flew out the window.

"Oh my God," he murmured, not certain if he intended that as a prayer for help or praise for the sight before him. Cody had grown used to Carina's white cotton nightgowns. He had found them endearing as well as innocently provocative.

The gown she now wore was anything but innocent. Made of material so sheer he could scarcely see it, the color was the same deep black as her eyes. Her coral-tipped nipples shone through the black lace at the top. The slightly darker circle of her navel was not concealed, nor was the thickly curled triangle at the top of her thighs. The gown opened on both sides from hem to waist, exposing the length of her leg and hip.

"Is that what you've been sleepin' in these days?" he asked, sounding hoarse. "It's a wonder you haven't died of pneumonia."

She came toward him, seemingly untroubled by his comments. She slipped under the covers and stretched out beside him. With a hint of a smile and a twinkle in her eyes, she said, "No one will ever see me in this but you, Cody."

He had to swallow before he managed to say, "I sure as hell hope not. I'd hate to have to kill a man at this stage in my life."

She turned so that she faced him, propping herself on one elbow. "I wanted you to find me sexy."

"If I found you any more sexy I'd explode," which was exactly what he thought he was going to do. He wasn't certain he could handle this kind of stimulation, not after the past year of celibacy. Reminding himself that he had just gotten out of the hospital, he carefully pulled her closer to his side and nuzzled her under her chin.

"Are we going to watch television?" she asked, in a voice filled with amusement.

He hit the off button of the remote without looking while placing kisses along the side of her neck. He heard her sigh and felt her touch him at the same time. Her touch sent him up in flames.

He placed his trembling hand on her thigh and felt the shimmering material that was the only thing between them. Sliding his hand along her leg he could feel the tiny ripples of sensation on her skin as the combination of smooth, silky material and roughened palm aroused her.

Once again, she ran her fingertips up and over his heated flesh.

"Where did you learn to do that?" he asked, remembering how shy she had been.

She gazed at him out of heavy-lidded eyes. "I read in a book that you're supposed to do what gives you pleasure and that sometimes the other person will gain pleasure from it as well."

"You enjoy touching me?"

He saw color flood her cheeks once more, and he grinned. Despite their time apart, she hadn't changed all that much.

She nodded her head, watching him with wide eyes. He studied her for a long moment, then said, "Okay. Then be my guest." With that he stretched out beside her and tugged her closer.

She looked at him, startled.

"Show me what else the book taught you," he coaxed, knowing his grin was more than a little wicked.

The smile quickly left him when she proceeded to follow his instructions with infinite attention to detail. "Oh—uh—Carina, honey. I can't handle that right now. It's been so—o-o-o-h—long and I don't want to—uh-uh-uh—o-o-h..."

Later he didn't remember when she carefully had straddled him without putting pressure on either wound. She seemed to hover above him, light as a butterfly, while he filled his hands and his mouth with her. He forgot about everything but the two of them together again. There were no more thoughts, only feelings . . . and what he felt encompassed a multitude of pleasurable sensations too numerous to count.

When he could no longer contain himself he stiffened and cried out, aware of her pulsing movement gripping him, draining him completely.

"What is it?" she panted, concern filling her eyes. "Are you hurt? Did we do something—"

He scarcely had the breath to laugh. "Yeah. I'd say we did something, all right." He waited for more air before he added, "My gently reared darling has turned into a tiger in bed."

She edged away from him, stretching out along his unwounded side. "Is that good?"

"Oh, *chula* . . . honey, it sure ain't bad!"

Cody woke up the next morning with a stripe of sunshine on his face. With a silent groan he stumbled out of bed and jerked the draperies closed, then felt his way back to bed.

Dimly he was aware that he hadn't obtained much sleep the night before. Technically speaking, he hadn't obtained *any* sleep the night before, because the sky had already lightened before he had fallen into an exhausted rest, his arms securely around Carina.

She hadn't stirred just now when he got up. Nor did she stir when he returned to bed and slipped beneath the covers. He leaned on his elbow and gazed down at her.

They were back together again and this time he was determined to keep them together. She had given up her job, a job he knew was important to her. They needed to discuss the future.

While he had been convalescing, he had asked Cole and Cameron what they thought about establishing a speech-therapy clinic in San Antonio. Both of them had been enthusiastic about the idea. So perhaps he had an anniversary present of his own.

When she opened her eyes and saw him watching her, she smiled. He had never seen anyone more beautiful.

"How are you feeling?" she asked.

"Content. At peace with my world. How are you feeling?"

"Very much the same. I was talking about your injuries."

"Considering all our activity last night, I feel surprisingly well rested." He yawned and leaned back on his pillows. Playing with one of her wispy curls that he found very endearing, he said, "I was watching you sleep and thinking about how much I love you and how scared I've been this past year that I was going to lose you. Thank God you chose to honor your marriage vows, even if they were made under protest."

"Cody! That isn't true. I was angry at Alfonso for forcing you to marry me. I had hoped that someday you would perhaps want to marry me, but I wanted it to be your decision." She shook her head. "I know you felt trapped, that you had never thought of me in that way. You were very honorable, marrying me under those circumstances."

He reached for her and pulled her in his arms. When she was arranged to his satisfaction, he said, "I want to tell you a story." He lifted her hand and placed a kiss on her ring finger.

"When my folks were killed, my whole world fell apart. I was angry with everybody and at everything. My life had changed in a way that I hated but could do nothing about. I remember one night, in particular.

My Aunt Letty came into my room late, hours after everyone else had gone to bed. I don't know how she knew I was still awake. At the time I think I was convinced she had X-ray vision eyes that could see through walls and across the miles. That lady never missed much." He placed a light kiss on Carina's nose. "Looking back, I realize that she probably checked on me every night without my knowing it.

"I was sitting on the window seat in my room staring out at the stars, wondering if maybe two of those stars might be my mom and dad. I didn't have a very clear idea of exactly where heaven was and how a person got there.

"I expected her to tell me to get to bed, that I had school the next day. Instead, she pulled up a chair and sat down beside me. She began to talk.

"Even now, I'm surprised at what she told me, because—as you well know—Letitia Callaway is one of the most unsentimental people you would ever hope to know. She started telling me about how my mom and dad met. She told their story as a sister watching her brother fall head-over-heels in love, courting a beautiful young girl. She told me about the time when her brother came home excited that his love had agreed to marry him.

"Then she reached into her pocket and pulled out an object. It was too dark for me to see what it was, but she held it on her palm and said, 'Your dad bought your mom the most gorgeous ring, ornately decorated with stones, and she told him that although she found the ring quite beautiful, she wouldn't be comfortable wearing it. Her hands were small and slim. So then he went out and bought her this,' my aunt told me and held out her hand.

"I felt something drop into my palm and I looked at it. It was a small gold filigree ring. I remember staring at it and hurting inside, real bad. The last time I had seen that ring my mama had been wearing it. She never took it off. Aunt Letty told me that she wanted me to have that ring to remind me of the wonderful love my parents had for each other and for the three of us boys. I remember her saying, 'Cole and Cameron were given a few more years to build memories of their parents than you had, Cody. You need something more tangible as a reminder. So keep this ring, knowing who it represents and what it represents.'"

Cody smoothed his palm across Carina's cheek. "Even at ten, I knew the tremendous gift my aunt had given me that night. She had given me back my belief in life and in the future. She had given me love in its most tangible form. I carried that ring with me until the day I placed it on your hand."

He took his thumb and gently wiped away one of the tears from her cheek, but more replaced it.

"Even when I didn't fully understand my feelings, I knew that somehow it was right for you to wear this ring." He lifted her hand and placed another kiss across her fingers. "This ring has always symbolized eternal love to me, and you were the embodiment of that love. I was too much of a coward to admit it for a long time."

"You are anything but a coward, Cody."

He shook his head. "Aunt Letty knew the minute she met you how I really felt about you. She knew because she saw that ring on your finger. She also knew that I had to give you your freedom or neither one of us would ever have a chance to be happy together."

Carina smiled. "She's quite a woman, isn't she?"

"The last of a dying breed. Tougher than a boot but she would do anything in the world for you. To her, family is *everything*."

"Family's important to me, too, Cody."

"I know, honey. That's why I'm so glad you've worked out your differences with Alfonso."

"What I mean is, a family of my own is important to me. That's why I was so devastated when I lost the baby."

In a quiet voice, Cody said, "I'm not saying that I wasn't upset about the miscarriage, because I was... sorry because of the baby and sorry that you had to go through all of that alone. I intend to spend the rest of my life making up for those lonely years we weren't together."

"Be careful what you promise, now. I might keep you so busy training horses and children that you'll dream of the days when you were a loner."

He pressed his lips against hers, paused and whispered, "Don't count on it," before his mouth found hers once more.

Epilogue

Cody sat with his feet propped up on the porch railing, his chair resting on the back two legs, and gazed out at the rolling hills around Cole's Austin home. Cole and Cameron were in similar positions on either side of him. Each of them was contemplating the fact that they had eaten entirely too much food off the recent Thanksgiving table and were now paying for it.

"The Cowboys played a hell of a game," Cameron said into the quiet surrounding them.

"Sure did," Cole agreed. "They'll make it to the Super Bowl this year for sure."

"You say that every year," Cody reminded his brother.

"So? They've got a strong team this year, better than I've seen in a long time."

Knowing what he was provoking, he said, "Well, if you ever get tired of backing the Cowboys, you might switch to the Oilers. They've been doing great this year."

"Wash your mouth out, boy," Cole growled, causing Cameron and Cody to laugh.

"You know," Cody said after another lengthy silence, "I think I actually miss not having Aunt Letty here, even though I'm sure she's enjoying her cruise. It just isn't the same, not having her point out all our shortcomings. Can't you just hear her, if she could see us now?" He pitched his voice into a falsetto. "'That's no way to sit in a chair. I didn't raise you to act like a bunch of heathens. You know how to behave.'"

"You sound just like her," Cameron said with a grin.

From behind them a soft, young voice said, "Daddy?" Three chairs hit the porch at the same time, three pairs of boots scraped the floor and three sets of eyes turned to see who wanted them.

Sherry Lynn Callaway came toddling toward them, her mother hovering just behind her. Cody swooped down and picked up his thirteen-month-old daughter. "Hello, precious," he cooed. "Did you have a good nap?" He glanced around and saw that his wife and both brothers were grinning at him like a bunch of fools.

"What's wrong with y'all?"

Cole cleared his throat, Cameron shuffled his feet and Carina patted his cheek. "Not a thing, Cody. Not a thing. Would you like to entertain your daughter? We've got a hot game of Spades going on inside."

"Sure," he said, settling back into his chair, this time with all four legs on the ground. He placed Sherry on his knee.

"They're really adorable at that age," Cole admitted, and nobody within hearing argued with him.

"I've been meaning to tell you," Cameron began slowly, "Janine and I are adopting a little boy."

"That's great, Cam," Cody said, rubbing his daughter's back.

"He's almost two. We told them that age didn't matter. I figure the only way I'm going to be able to keep up with you two is to get 'em on the hoof, so to speak."

"Hey," Cody replied, "Don't look at me. We were married almost four years before we started our family."

Cole gave Cody a lopsided grin. "Hell, son, it just took you that long to figure out what you were supposed to be doing."

"You feel safe with me sitting here with my hands full."

Cameron chimed in. "You have to admit that once you got the hang of things you haven't wasted much time. Clay's barely three, Sherry just turned one and Carina is pregnant again."

Cody grinned. "Can't argue with the facts, can I?"

"Trisha is excited at the idea of having a baby brother," Cam went on. "She wants several more. I'm sure so that she can boss them around."

Cole looked out over the hills. "The folks would be proud to see the families we're raising. I just wish they could have seen us the way we were today all gathered around the table."

"I don't know about you, but I hear myself talking to one of the kids and I sound just like Dad used to," Cody said. "I guess that's part of being family, repeating the same stories, passing on the sayings."

"They taught us about love," Cam said thoughtfully. "It was a lesson worth learning."

Cody glanced over his shoulder and saw that Carina had come to the door again, no doubt to check on her daughter. With his heart in his eyes he answered his brother without taking his eyes off his wife.

"And worth waiting for," he added softly.

*   *   *   *   *

VOWS
A series celebrating marriage
by Sherryl Woods

To Love, Honor and Cherish—these were the words that three generations of Halloran men promised their women they'd live by. But these vows made in love are each challenged by the tests of time....

In October—Jason Halloran meets his match in *Love* #769;
In November—Kevin Halloran rediscovers love—with his wife—in *Honor* #775;
In December—Brandon Halloran rekindles an old flame in *Cherish* #781.

These three stirring tales are coming down the aisle toward you—only from Silhouette Special Edition!

SILHOUETTE® Desire™

MAN OF THE MONTH

YOU'VE ASKED FOR IT, YOU'VE GOT IT! MAN OF THE MONTH: 1992

ONLY FROM SILHOUETTE DESIRE

You just couldn't get enough of them, those men from Silhouette Desire—twelve sinfully sexy, delightfully devilish heroes. Some will make you sweat, some will make you sigh . . . but every long, lean one of them will have you swooning. So here they are, *more* of the men we couldn't resist bringing to you for one more year. . . .

BEST MAN FOR THE JOB
by Dixie Browning in June

MIDNIGHT RIDER
by Cait London in July

CONVENIENT HUSBAND
by Joan Hohl in August

NAVARRONE
by Helen R. Myers in September

A MAN OF HONOR
by Paula Detmer Riggs in October

BLUE SKY GUY
by Carole Buck in November

IT HAD TO BE YOU
by Jennifer Greene in December

Don't let these men get away! MAN OF THE MONTH, only in Silhouette Desire!

MOM92JD

Silhouette
R O M A N C E™

═══ HEARTLAND ═══
HOLIDAYS

Christmas bells turn into wedding bells for the Gallagher siblings in Stella Bagwell's *Heartland Holidays* trilogy.

THEIR FIRST THANKSGIVING (#903) in November
Olivia Westcott had once rejected Sam Gallagher's proposal—
and in his stubborn pride, he'd refused to hear her reasons why.
Now Olivia is back...and it is about time Sam Gallagher listened!

THE BEST CHRISTMAS EVER (#909) in December
Soldier Nick Gallagher had come home to be the best man at his
brother's wedding—not to be a groom! But when he met single
mother Allison Lee, he knew he'd found his bride.

NEW YEAR'S BABY (#915) in January
Kathleen Gallagher had given up on love and marriage until she
came to the rescue of neighbor Ross Douglas...and the newborn
baby he'd found on his doorstep!

Come celebrate the holidays with Silhouette Romance!

AMERICAN HERO

Every month in Silhouette Intimate Moments, one fabulous, irresistible man is featured as an American Hero. You won't want to miss a single one. Look for them wherever you buy books, or follow the instructions below and have these fantastic men mailed straight to your door!

In September:
MACKENZIE'S MISSION by Linda Howard, IM #445

In October:
BLACK TREE MOON by Kathleen Eagle, IM #451

In November:
A WALK ON THE WILD SIDE by Kathleen Korbel, IM #457

In December:
CHEROKEE THUNDER by Rachel Lee, IM #463

AMERICAN HEROES—men you'll adore, from authors you won't want to miss. Only from Silhouette Intimate Moments.

To order your copies of the AMERICAN HERO titles above, please send your name, address, zip or postal code, along with a check or money order for $3.39 for each book ordered (please do not send cash), plus 75¢ postage and handling ($1.00 in Canada), payable to Silhouette Books, to:

In the U.S.

Silhouette Books
3010 Walden Avenue
P.O. Box 1396
Buffalo, NY 14269-1396

In Canada

Silhouette Books
P.O. Box 609
Fort Erie, Ontario
L2A 5X3

Please specify book title(s) with your order.
Canadian residents add applicable federal and provincial taxes.

IMHERO2

SILHOUETTE® Desire™

presents
SONS OF TEXAS
by Annette Broadrick

As rugged as their native land, the Callaway brothers—Cole, Cameron and Cody—are three sinfully sexy heroes ready to ride into your heart.

In September—
LOVE TEXAS STYLE! (SD#734)

In October—
COURTSHIP TEXAS STYLE! (SD#739)

In November—
MARRIAGE TEXAS STYLE! (SD#745)

Don't let these Sons of Texas get away—men as hot as the Texas sun they toil . . . and *romance* . . . under! Only from Silhouette Desire . . .